Sammy and the Devil Dog

To Reese,
Happy Reading!
Susan Bran

Sammy and
the Devil Dog

by

Susan Brown

Yellow Farmhouse Publications

Sammy and the Devil Dog
ISBN-13 Print Edition: 978-1544799353
ISBN-10 Print Edition: 1544799357

Yellow Farmhouse Publications, Lake Stevens, WA, USA
Copyright © 2017
Publication Date: September 2017

This is a work of fiction. Names, characters, places and incidents are either the product of the author's imagination or are used fictitiously, and any resemblance to actual persons, living or dead, business establishments, events or locales is entirely coincidental.

Excerpt from *Not Yet Summer* © 2017 by Susan Brown
Excerpt from *Dragons of Frost and Fire* © 2015 by Susan Brown

Cover and Interior Design: Heather McIntyre
Cover&Layout, www.coverandlayout.com

Cover Photography: Girl © BestPhotoStudio
Dog © Anna Andersson Fotografi

This book is dedicated to

The people I love:

Past, Present, and Future

You know who you are.

Other books by Susan Brown you might enjoy

Not Yet Summer
Hey, Chicken Man!
Something's Fishy at Ash Lake
An Amber & Elliot Mystery
written with Anne Stephenson

Also try Susan Brown's fantasy books!

Dragons of Frost and Fire
Dragons of Desert and Dust

Coming soon!

Dragons of Wind and Waves	*March 2018*
Catching Toads	*May 2018*
You're Dead, David Borelli	*Fall 2018*
Pirates, Prowlers and Cherry Pie	*2018*
Twelve, *a mythic fantasy*	*2018*

Sammy and the Devil Dog

Contents

Chapter 1

Let's See You Dance!

Sammy sat motionless, or as near to motionless as it was possible for her. Her eyes hardly left the house phone sitting on the kitchen counter. Eleven minutes before her mom came home. If the call didn't come before then, Sammy was dead...or maybe worse than dead.

Impatiently Sammy shoved her bangs out of her eyes. The movement made the bruise on her shoulder ache a little more, but she didn't care. She glanced at the clock. Nine minutes. Maybe the traffic would be bad. Maybe her mom would be delayed. Mrs. Martinez didn't have her mom's cell phone number, so the call would come here. Maybe this time Sammy would be lucky.

Lucky...not likely....

Six minutes.

Then, shattering the silence, the phone rang. Holding her breath, Sammy waited, counting the rings...*one...two...three...four....* The answering machine picked up. *"Hi there. Sammy and Linda are dying to talk to you, but we aren't here! Leave a message. Leave a number. We'll call back!"*

"Hello, this is Tony from the Take a Stand Foundation. We're calling today..."

Sammy grabbed the receiver, held it at arms length for about three seconds and then slammed it down again. Silence. She looked at the clock.

Four minutes. Sammy drummed her fingers on the side of the table, and then lifted her head like a dog catching a distant sound.

"Oh no," she whispered. The painful rumble of her mom's old car turned into the long gravel drive.

"Oh, dirty dog, call now," she whispered, "Mrs. Martinez, call now...call now...!"

The phone rang. *One...two...three...four....*

"Hi there. Sammy and Linda are dying to talk to you, but we aren't here! Leave a message. Leave a number. We'll call back!"

The rumbling engine suddenly stopped. The car door squealed open....

"Hello Ms. Connor. This is Jeanne Martinez, principal at Samantha's school. I'm afraid that Samantha was involved in another incident today. I'd like to schedule a meeting with you

and your daughter to see what we can do to help Samantha improve her behavior. I know there have been a lot of changes in your lives recently, but we can't allow her to continue to make such inappropriate choices. Please call me to schedule a time."

The message machine beeped. Sammy jabbed the erase button as Linda Connor pushed open the kitchen door.

"Hi Sammy, how was school?" her mom asked. "Can you help me with these bags? I can't believe how much I saved at the consignment store. I found the cutest top! I told you I had a date Saturday with a guy I met at the pottery sale, didn't I?"

When Sammy took the largest bag, her mom pulled a bright pink blouse from the other stuffed plastic bag and held it up to her chin. "What do you think?"

"It's great, mom," Sammy said. "Really a good color on you."

Her mom grinned. "Thanks, kiddo. I'm going to get cleaned up and get some work done in my studio. What are you up to?"

"Erin got back from Japan on Tuesday, so we're going to hang out," Sammy said. "Is that okay?"

Her mom was already pulling off her outer clothes before heading to the shower, but she stopped and gave Sammy a squeeze. "I'm really glad she's back. This has been a tough time for you to be by yourself, without your best friend."

Sammy hugged back. "You too."

Her mom laughed a little shakily, and ran her fingers through her hair. "That's life," she said. "It just keeps on happening whether you're ready or not. I need to get cleaned up."

Sammy smiled like the good kid she used to be, until her mom was out of sight. Then she took the house phone off its cradle, turned it on, and dropped it to the floor. In a smooth motion, she nudged it behind and under the counter.

"And stay there," Sammy said.

Problem dealt with, Sammy ran out back to get her bike. She and Erin were meeting at the convenience store. When Sammy had puffed her way up the long hill, Erin was waiting for her outside the store with two big freezies in her hands. When she tried to wave with the cups in her hand, it looked so funny, Sammy started to laugh.

Jumping off, Sammy propped her bike against the wall and took a long frozen slurp, so cold it almost burned. "Oh," she sighed blissfully, "you will be my best friend forever."

Erin giggled, took a long swallow herself, and then looked at her friend seriously.

"Did your mom understand that you couldn't help that fight?" she demanded. "That the girls were making that little kid cry by teasing him?"

"Sure," Sammy said jerking the straw up and down. "My mom's great that way."

Erin frowned. "She didn't used to be," she said slowly. "You used to always go to your grandpa."

"Well," Sammy's voice had a weird scratch to it, "he's not here so I guess she just picked it up instead."

"Oh Sammy," Erin cried. "I am such a bad friend. I am so sorry. I shouldn't have said anything. Don't be sad!"

Her eyes held such pleading that Sammy forced herself to laugh. "It's okay," she said. "Come on – let's ride somewhere."

"Your house," Erin said. "I haven't seen it."

"Yes, you have," Sammy said.

"But not when you lived there," Erin said earnestly. "I'll bet it's entirely different now. And special because you're there."

"You're going to be disappointed," Sammy said, getting back on her bike. She didn't want to go home, but then she thought of the phone under the cupboard. Her mom would be out of the shower by now, and might notice it wasn't there. And Sammy really wanted to stay out of trouble for awhile. Last week her mom had been so mad when Sammy got blamed for wrecking the class field trip – she just hadn't realized everyone had already gotten on the bus.

Glumly, Sammy leaned back on the bike, pushed off and slowly coasted away from the store letting gravity do all the work while she sipped her drink and lightly steered with one hand.

Aaw-oooo-oooo.

Sammy must have imagined the noise – it didn't belong in the trim suburb by the convenience store.

Aaw-oooo-oooo. A dog howl, mournful and low. Alone. Lonely.

Sammy jerked her head around, nearly lost her balance and just in time, swerved out of the way of a car. Her freezie spun across the road in a fizzing whirl.

Honk! The woman glared as she sped past.

"You don't own the road!" Sammy shouted. She smacked her hands on the handlebars. Erin, completely unaware, coasted down the hill.

Aaw-oooo-oooo.

Weird. This was weird. Sammy pushed back her helmet, trying to hear better. Animal cries, whimpering. And then....

Bang! Bang! Bang! Bangbangbang!

A dog yelped and cried. Laughter exploded through the air.

Sammy dropped her bike on the grass curb. The noises came from the yard that backed onto the sidewalk. A chain link fence, thick with vines, blocked her view.

The dog's cry rose again then trailed away.

Without hesitating, Sammy toe-climbed to the top of the fence. In a weedy back yard, two teenage boys were laughing so hard they could hardly stand up. A black and white dog, long-legged and shaggy, was nearly strangling himself trying to escape the chain that held him to a tree. A litter of red paper fluttered across the beaten dirt. The smell of gunpowder snagged Sammy's nostrils.

"Hey, dummy!" the tallest boy yelled to the dog. "Let's see you dance."

He held up a string of red firecrackers, struck a match, and lit the fuse. The boy threw them at the dog. The animal whimpered, leaped frantically into the air, then fell heavily as the chain nearly choked him. The crackers hissed and sputtered near his face.

"Stop!" Sammy screamed.

She leapt down from the fence and raced across the yard. The fuse was almost gone when Sammy kicked.

The first cracker went off as her toe hit the pack. She felt the smack and heard the pop. But the rest of the string flew in smooth arc back toward the boys.

"Hey!" they howled as the firecrackers popped and banged at their feet.

"How do you like dancing!" Sammy tore over to them. Firecrackers, big ones, were going off in her brain. "How could you do that? You are wicked and cruel and you deserve to die!"

"Ah shut up, you little witch!" the shorter boy snarled.

The biggest one leaned against the wall and grinned. "We weren't hurting it. But that was a good move, kid. Real good kick."

"Get off our property!" The first one glared.

"Not a chance!" Sammy jabbed her fists into her hips. "I'm going to call the police and they're going to arrest you for cruelty to animals. You were torturing that dog!"

"What torture," the tallest teenager demanded. "We're training our dog to be a watchdog. And a watchdog is no good unless it's mean."

"You're just hurting it. You can't do that!"

"Yes we can – it's our dog."

Sammy narrowed her eyes and tried to decide if she had any chance of survival if she smacked that superior grin right off his face.

What would Papa Jack have done?

"Sammy?" Erin was hanging onto the fence, peering over the top. "What's going on? Are you okay?"

"Yes, but those jerks were throwing fire crackers at him." Sammy turned to the animal. The dog was trying to hide behind the tree, pulling on his chain, making soft yelping noises. "Oh, you poor thing..."

She walked slowly toward it, holding out her hand. "He's just a puppy!" At the sound of her voice, the dog swiveled so that it crouched, nose pointing toward her.

"Oh you beautiful thing," Sammy crooned. The sun shone on the dog's rich black coat and gleamed on the long white diamond on his forehead. His two front paws and the thick ruff on his chest were clean white too. Sammy crouched and held out her hand. The dog sprang at her.

Sammy leaped back, tripped and fell. The dog stood over her, snarling. Black eyes ringed with white; black lips curled above white fangs. Sammy couldn't move, didn't dare move.

And then another boy ran past, grabbed the dog's chain and hauled him off. The dog barked and snapped.

"Shut up!" The boy smacked the dog on the head. The dog whimpered again and dropped down, head on its too-big puppy paws. The wild black eyes warmed to brown. The edge of a soft pink tongue peeked between its lips.

Sammy sat up. "Brian? Brian Haydon? What are you doing here?"

"I live here, stupid."

Sammy scrambled to her feet. "Here? I thought you lived in the apartments."

Brian shrugged. "We moved. That's why I got a dog. But he isn't any good."

Sammy took a deep breath, making the world look normal again. The pup's white-tipped tail thumped once.

"Do you know what they were doing to him?" Sammy demanded.

Brian looked up at the teenagers leaning against the wall. His face got hard. "Joe, I'm training the dog. You probably ruined him."

"Aah, what a shame," the big one, Joe, said. "You're such a woos, Brian. Besides we didn't hurt him – much. Com'on Kyle. Play you, *Die Again Sucka,* on the computer."

They banged into the house. Brian swore under his breath.

"Who are *they*?" Erin hopped down from the fence, careful to keep a long way from the dog. She pushed her helmet more securely onto her dark hair.

"My brothers." Brian's voice had a snarl in it, kind of like the dog.

"It's against the law to abuse a dog," Erin told him. "You can't do that."

"I don't abuse him," Brian muttered.

"You just hit him on the head," Sammy retorted.

Brian scowled. "You have to be strict with a dog or he won't know who his master is."

"No! Not that strict," Sammy insisted.

She walked as close as she dared to the dog. He lifted his head and growled deep in his throat. "It's okay," she said softly. "Can't you tell I'm your friend?" The dog stared at her. His tail thumped again. He cocked his head.

"What kind of dog is he?" Sammy asked.

"Mutt," Brian said. "Got him from a guy down the street when he was a puppy."

The kids studied the dog who stared back at them. "I think he's part lab," Erin said. "He's black like a lab."

"He's too big," Brian scoffed.

"And his fur is too long," Sammy agreed. "And he has white on his chest."

The dog's head lifted a little more, and this time his tail really thumped.

She crouched down, flipped her hair from her eyes, and leaned toward the dog. "You want to be friendly, don't you boy?" She held out her hand, back first, fingers curled down.

The dog stood up. His tail straightened behind him.

"Good boy," she whispered.

Quicker than she could see, he leaped. She felt his hot breath, heard the snarl in his throat and glimpsed his sharp white teeth as they closed on her bare arm.

"No!" Sammy cried. "Bad dog!"

In the background she was aware of Erin shrieking. Furious, Sammy leaned closer to the dog's face. His teeth pressed painfully on her arm and his growl was low and steady.

"You let go," she said. "You be a good dog and let go."

She felt as though her eyes had a thin line of energy connecting directly to the dog's deep brown ones. The growl rumbled slowly. The jaws tightened a little, teeth not yet breaking the skin, but soon...

"I'm not the bad guy," she whispered through gritted teeth. "I'm nice. You don't have to bite me and we can be friends. You need a friend."

The dog blinked, then suddenly yelped. Brian hauled him back roughly by the collar, and smacked him on the head again. The dog growled and bared his teeth.

"You stupid, no good dog," the boy berated him. "Drop it!" *Whack.* He smacked the dog again.

The dog backed up, lips curled and teeth gleaming in a deep snarl.

"Stop it!" Sammy yelled. "Don't you hit that dog again!"

Brian shook his head. "You got to be tough with a dog. Look how big and strong he is already. And he's only five months old. My Dad says he's a real devil. If I don't make him scared of me, what's going to make him do what I say?"

"Dogs do what you tell them because they love you!" Erin protested tearfully. "My golden retriever, Casey, does everything I tell her and she doesn't growl at me either. She loves me. She'd die for me."

Brian shrugged. "Jack was a real cute puppy. He slept with me until Dad said he had to be chained up out here and get turned into a watch dog."

Sammy thrust her chin forward. "If you hurt this dog again we'll report it to the police and you'll all get fined and go to jail."

Brian got a hard look on his face. "Ooh, I'm scared."

"I've warned you." Sammy headed to the fence, rubbing her arm. Bluish-purple tooth marks indented her skin and a line of pain crept past her elbow. The dog stared at her unblinking. "So long, boy," she said.

It took about two seconds to scramble over the fence. She rubbed her arm again. There was going to be a bruise but the dog hadn't broken the skin. He could have, couldn't he, if he wanted to? Maybe the dog didn't really want to hurt her.

"Do you think we should call the police?" Erin interrupted her thoughts.

"Maybe." Sammy picked up her bike from the grass. "Brian will beat us up at school."

"Oh, he wouldn't, because we're girls," Erin insisted.

"That's never stopped him before," Sammy said.

Brian was about six inches taller, twice as heavy and three times as strong as any other kid at Carr Elementary. When anyone, any age or size bugged him, he punched them out. Once, he'd shoved the PE teacher and pulled a five days suspension.

"Brian is disgusting – disgusting and weird." Erin tightened her helmet strap and pushed off, gliding smoothly down the bike lane.

Sammy looked back at the fence, wondering what the dog was doing now. What had Brian called him? She froze. *Jack!* The dog's name was Jack. Sammy bit her lip and pedaled slowly after her friend.

"How could Brian name his dog Jack?" she demanded.

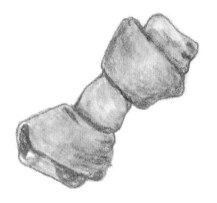

Chapter 2

No One Wants a Vicious Dog

"You know," Erin said, "this house has a great yard. I mean look at how big it is."

The two girls wheeled their bikes up the rutted gravel drive toward Sammy's new home. It had belonged to Papa Jack's family forever but until two months ago, Sammy, her mom and Papa Jack lived in a big, pale grey house by the golf course. This one had been rented out.

"The yard's full of blackberry brambles," Sammy said. "Why don't we just go to your house?"

"Because we're going to yours," Erin answered. "I've been gone since June! You can't keep me away now!" She gave her bike another push and bumped along toward the house.

Erin had left the last day of school to visit her Japanese grandparents. It wasn't her friend's fault she'd been gone through the awful time, but acting like nothing was different made a sharp pain of grief clench in Sammy's chest, like she couldn't breathe. Like everything else, that made her angry. But Erin was her friend, probably her only friend now, so Sammy didn't want her to guess how mad she was inside.

"Wait up," Sammy called.

The one-story house wasn't much more than a rambling cottage set back about fifty yards from the road. Papa Jack had worked each weekend to rebuild the long porch three years ago. Sammy had helped.

The smell of fresh-cut pine, hot summer bodies, and Papa Jack's after-shave had blended in her nostrils. Her job was to steady the boards while he sawed. Then she held the nails ready. Clean silver nails, lumber smells, and the *bam bam* of a hammer meant something wonderful could be made with bare hands.

When the last nail was driven in, she and her grandpa sat on the porch steps, side by side, each drinking a bottle of cold 7-Up.

She wouldn't think about that. Sammy jammed her bike over the stones and leaned it against the greying porch. The renters were supposed to have painted it, but they didn't. The unopened paint cans were still stacked in a corner of the barn.

Erin stepped back about ten feet and slowly surveyed the whole place.

"This could be really cute," she said finally. "But I don't understand why you moved from your other house?"

"Bills," Sammy said briefly. "It costs a lot of money to be in the hospital and nursing home as long as Papa Jack was. More than the insurance would pay. Mom had to sell the other house to get the money."

"Couldn't you have sold this one?" Erin asked.

Sammy shook her head. "No one wanted to buy it and Mom needs the barn for her ceramics studio."

"It'll be really cute," Erin said again, "once you get it fixed up."

"I'm going to fix it up," Sammy told her. "A lot. Papa Jack taught me how to do a lot of stuff."

"It'll be really great," Erin said. Sammy smiled. Erin always said good things – even if it was a stretch of the imagination.

The girls went around back to where the old barn crouched under a thriving scramble of blackberries. A rusting, tipped-over washing machine and a tumbled brick barbecue made a hollow in the bushes. Erin picked a couple of berries still clinging to the canes and popped them in her mouth.

Sammy pushed open the heavy barn door. "Hi, Mom."

Linda Connor, hair damp and wispy from the heat, smiled across the cluttered room. Rough shelves held stacks of pottery and clay sculptures in all stages of completion. Two greyish-coated pottery wheels sat on the cement floor in the center of the room. Buckets of clay and water squatted beside them. At the back, in what had once been a horse stall, the kiln door was open. Sammy could see the white and blue sheen of a large, inlaid bowl her mom had been working on all week.

"Oh, Ms. Connor," Erin breathed. "That's so gorgeous."

Sammy's mom's smile widened. "I'm pleased with it," she said. "It's great to see you back, Erin. Sammy's missed you. It's been a rough few months for us."

"I guess," Erin said. "I'm really sorry about your father." Her lip trembled a little.

"Thank you, sweetie. We're really missing him." She went back to the stall and began fussing with the kiln.

Sammy took a deep breath. "Mom, can we make cookies?"

"Good idea. There isn't a whole lot in the kitchen to nibble on."

As they headed into the house, Sammy took a close look at the porch. It would need washing too, but paint would make it look a lot better. While Erin used the bathroom, Sammy took her mom's wallet out of her purse and silently checked to see how much money her mom had. Two dollars. Not enough for even a paintbrush. Did that mean two dollars was all they had until... when? Papa Jack's monthly pension checks stopped coming when he died. Sammy bit her lip. Where was her mom going to get money?

When the bills came from the doctors and labs and hospital and hospice and funeral home, her mom had used up everything Papa Jack had saved. Next she'd sold Papa Jack's car with the soft leather seats and the smell of him all through it. She'd come back with an old beater of a car that smelled sour and had a scraped fender. Then some of the nice furniture and the big dining room table had gone out the door.

Finally, she had sold the big grey house on the golf course. Her mom had had the studio fixed up with heavy-duty wiring and a new kiln – but that couldn't be worth a whole house. There had to be some money in the bank still...didn't there?

"I should call my mom," Erin interrupted Sammy's thoughts. As her friend used her own cell phone to report home, Sammy guiltily shoved the wallet back into the purse. Erin didn't notice. While calling, she'd bumped closed the swinging door that separated the kitchen from living room.

"Did I break it?" Erin asked, sliding her phone into her pocket with one hand and trying to make the door stay back against the kitchen wall with the other. The heavy wood kept whooshing shut again, slamming anyone in its way.

Sammy caught the door's edge and shook her head. "No, the catch doesn't work right, and this door just looks for a chance to wham someone."

Erin giggled. "Kind of like a watch door?"

Sammy laughed. "Having nothing to steal, we picked the cheap alarm system. The door attacks strangers."

They got it propped open again, finally. "If you had a doorstop, it would stay put," Erin said.

"I guess. Do you want to stay for dinner?" Sammy asked. She made a face. "Scrambled eggs and macaroni and cheese."

Erin grinned. "And chocolate chip cookies."

"And then the dog bit Sammy," Erin told

Sammy's mom. "I think we should call the police."

Linda turned to her daughter. "You didn't say the dog bit you!"

Sammy shifted uncomfortably in the wooden chair, reached for the bowl of macaroni and cheese, and spooned some onto her plate. "We should call the police because of what they were doing to that poor dog. It was horrible."

"How could you prove anything?" her mother asked. "They would want some kind of proof."

"We could tell them what we saw."

"We'd swear to it," Erin said earnestly.

"Then they'd have to stop hurting it," Sammy insisted.

Her mom shrugged. "We could try, but I bet they'd just take the dog away and destroy it."

"What!" Sammy put down her fork. "That isn't fair. It isn't the dog's fault! It's only a puppy anyway."

Her mother nodded. "I know. But no one wants a vicious dog."

"I would, and it wasn't vicious," Sammy protested. "If it was, it would have bit me a lot harder. See, it didn't even break the skin." She held out her arm.

"Yeeouch," her mom said. "I don't want a dog around that would leave a bruise like that."

Sammy jabbed her fork into the macaroni. "If it was a truly bad, evil dog, it would have bitten me through to the bone and I would be dying of rabies."

"Not until after dinner." Her mom picked up her plate and carried it to the sink. "Now, did you girls bake some cookies or did you just gorge yourselves on batter?"

"Oh, Ms. Connor," Erin giggled. "We baked most of them."

She got up and carried her plate to the sink and gave it to Sammy's mom to be rinsed. Sammy stayed at her chair, stirring macaroni into the scrambled eggs. There was a story Papa Jack had told her...

"Mom, do you remember the dog Papa Jack had when he was little?"

Her mother plopped a plate of cookies on the table and helped herself to one. "Not exactly. It was before I was born."

Sammy made a face but kept going. "His dad found a dog that was half-starved and had marks on it like someone was beating it."

Her mom looked at her sharply.

Sammy went on talking before her mom could interrupt. "He took the dog home and named him Dexter. And then Dexter became a really good dog after a while and really loved Papa Jack's father. Then a year later this guy came pounding at the door. It was his dog, he said. He'd been here hunting the year before but the dog ran away, and now he wanted Dexter back."

Sammy took a breath. She wished she could tell a story like Papa Jack, slow and full of details so everybody could see it in their heads.

"I remember the story now," her mother said. "Didn't the dog go hide under the bed when it heard the man's voice?"

"Yes!" Sammy said. "That's what convinced Great Grandpa that it really was the man's dog – and that he should never give him back."

"Oh no. He didn't, did he?" Erin looked really worried. She could always be counted on to feel sorry for anything that was hurt.

Sammy's mom wasn't so easily convinced. She raised her eyebrows. "I think I'm getting your point."

"Great Grandpa wouldn't give him back. He let Dexter stay under the bed." Sammy punctuated this part of the story with her fork. "He gave the man ten dollars for Dexter and Papa Jack said that was a lot of money then."

"It surely was," Sammy's mom said, "but honey, there's a difference between then and now."

"What difference?"

"We didn't find the dog wandering loose, we haven't kept it for a year, and most important, I don't have a spare ten dollars."

"Great Grandpa never had any extra money either," Sammy argued. "Papa Jack said they were dirt poor."

Her mother took another cookie. "Not dirt poor. They grew food in that dirt and made almost everything else." She took Sammy's hand and squeezed it.

"But it was here. In this house."

Her mother shrugged. "That was then; this is now. Things are different for us."

The fields that Great Grandpa and Papa Jack had farmed were covered with a golf course and fancy houses. The old farm garden was a thicket of blackberries. But what her mother really meant, Sammy knew, was that her mom didn't have a job and her pottery and sculptures didn't make much money. And besides, her mom never seemed to care about Papa Jack's stories.

"We can wash up," Erin was telling Sammy's Mom. "If you need to do more work."

"That's really sweet of you, Erin," Linda said.

"Oh please," Sammy rolled her eyes. "I do the dishes every night."

Erin grinned. "I know, but we didn't finish all the batter, did we?"

The teacher, Mrs. Bennett, was passing out test papers and Sammy was trying to write down the correct answers. But the room seemed shadowy and she could hear firecrackers in the distance. And now she could hear crying...a funny kind of crying. Mournful and pleading, like someone all alone and thinking they were going to be all alone forever. Sammy lifted her head and looked out the window. The black dog with the white bib had his paws up on the outside ledge and was looking in. Such sad eyes. And he was making the crying, mourning sound.

Sammy looked around the room. No one else seemed to hear the cries but Papa Jack. He was in the corner, fixing the hinges on the door.

"Papa Jack!" He turned around and looked at her, surprised, his concentration broken from his fixing.

Sammy ran across the room to him and flung herself in his arms. He held her in a strong, warm hug. She had almost forgotten what his hugs felt like. She had to hold on to him forever, because there wouldn't be another hug.

"Now Sammy Jay," he said, "you're not crying, are you? I told you we'd always be together. Always!"

Sammy tried to hold on, but like air sliding from her arms, Papa Jack turned away and picked up his tools. "I was laid up too long. There are a lot of things that need attention."

Sammy looked across the room at the dog, still pressed against the window. "I'll help, Papa Jack."

She turned around again and Papa Jack was gone. Only his yellow handled screwdriver and hammer, brown and smooth from use, lay on the table beside the door.

"Oh Papa Jack," Sammy cried. She wrapped her arms around herself, trying to make the same warm safety of her grandfather.

As she slid down to the floor, arms around herself, she slid out of sleep. Her eyes were dripping tears in the dark room. Sammy stuffed her blankets into her mouth so she wouldn't sob out loud.

She remembered how as he lay in the hospital bed, barely conscious, Papa Jack had roused himself because she was crying. She'd tried to be brave and cheerful, but she couldn't help it. He had managed to lift his thin arm and put it on her shoulders.

"Ah Sammy, you're crying. Don't you know we'll be together always? Always." And then he slid back into the drugged sleep. She had hugged him, carefully so she wouldn't hurt the ribs that had broken from the cancer. She was sure, even in the awful sleep, that he had smiled at her.

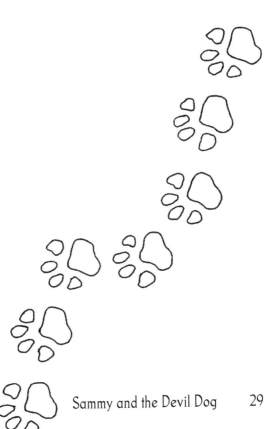

Sammy and the Devil Dog   29

30   Susan Brown

Chapter 3

His Name is Jack

Sammy carried her bowl and a box of Cheerios to the table, pouring as she went. Her mom was propped up, bleary-eyed over a cup of coffee.

"Morning, sweetie," she murmured.

"Morning. There was something I forgot to tell you about that dog," Sammy said.

"Hmm. What was that?"

Sammy sat down across from her mom and leaned her elbows on the table. "His name is Jack."

Her mom frowned. Obviously she didn't get it.

"Jack," Sammy said impatiently. "It's like Papa Jack and the story and his name is Jack. And," she rushed on before her mother could say anything, "and I dreamed about him and Papa Jack last night. I'm going to get that dog and I'm going to keep him."

"That's not a good idea, Sammy."

"I don't care. I have to. He can sleep in my room and I'll earn money to pay for his food myself. I'm going to look after everything. It's all taken care of."

"You sound just like my father when you talk like that." Her mom took a deep drink of coffee. "But remember that it's entirely your responsibility – not mine."

Sammy just nodded, spooned up her cereal, dumped the bowl into the sink and went to her room for her backpack.

When she returned to the kitchen, it was empty. Through the back window, she could see her mom, coffee mug in hand, opening the studio door. Sammy darted to the fridge, took a piece of sliced ham, and put it in a plastic bag.

Then she raced for her bike and took off toward Brian's house.

She left the bike leaning against the fence, climbed up and looked over. The dog was straining toward her against his short leash. Once again his lips were pulled back in a rumbling growl. He looked really fierce. A shiver of fear went through her. Like a dog herself, she shook her head and shoulders to clear the fright away.

For a moment Sammy just stared down at the dog. The rumble grew noisier. She could see that his food dish was empty and dead leaves floated in the scummy water dish.

"Poor thing," Sammy whispered. She wondered if she dared climb down and look for fresh water for the dog.

The snarl suddenly raged into a bark. Sammy winced.

Devil dog....

"Quiet, boy. Be quiet, Jack." She spoke loudly, hoping the dog wouldn't hear the quaver in her voice. Dogs could smell fear, couldn't they? Well, she'd just better not let herself be afraid.

The dog slipped back to the low, rumbly growl again. The sun shone over his black coat, glistening softly. His tail was mostly straight up, but the breeze ruffled the plume a little. Sammy looked deeply into the dog's brown eyes and tried to connect again.

"I'm your friend, Jack. We have to be friends because you're going to be my dog. I'm going to be in charge – not because I'll be mean to you, but because I'm going to be nicer to you than anyone in your life has ever been. And just to show you, I brought you some ham. You'll like that ham, won't you boy..."

Slowly, Sammy took out the bag and, balancing on the fence, took out the meat. The dog's ears pricked up and he made a little whimpering sound. Was he hungry? Did Brian feed him enough? She should have brought the whole package.

"Here boy," Sammy said softly. She tore the meat in half and tossed one piece toward Jack. He leapt against the chain, nearly choking, but managed to grab the meat. In one gulp it was down his throat.

"Oh, good dog," Sammy told him. The tail waved just a little. "Here's the rest." This time Sammy made sure the meat was thrown well into the dog's reach. She didn't want him to hurt himself.

"That's a good dog," she said. "I'll see you later."

She jumped backwards off the fence and landed lightly on her toes. Behind the fence, Jack started barking. Sammy hesitated then pushed off on her bicycle. If Brian or his brothers came out to see what was happening, she didn't want them to see her. They were so mean, they'd probably tie the dog out of reach, just for spite.

Sammy gripped the handlebars tightly. She couldn't let them hurt the dog any more. She would solve the problem. Everything would be okay.

The rest of the ride she imagined herself with Jack – throwing a Frisbee, going for walks, patting him, burying her face in his soft fur. And all the while Jack would be panting happily, looking at her with love and approval, knowing that she was the one who could fix everything.

She was still a block away when she heard the bell ring.

"Not again!" she groaned. Her teacher, Mrs. Bennett, had said if Sammy was late one more time, she'd have to go to the office before coming to class.

Sammy wheeled her bike into the parking lot, dodged a car that was dropping off some other late kids and slammed her bike into the rack. Hastily, she wound the chain through the spokes and smacked the lock shut. Without a pause, she raced through the doors and veered toward her classroom.

"Samantha Connor!" Mrs. Haines, the librarian eyed her over the top of her classes. "Please walk in the halls."

Sammy forced a smile and slowed her legs into a stiff walk.

"*Good morning, students!*" The PA crackled to life.

Sammy groaned again and slid into her classroom. Frank was standing at the front of the class with the lunch count and attendance pad.

We have a few announcements this morning. The service club will meet in Mr. Evan's room at lunch...

"Sammy, you're late!" Frank declared. Mrs. Bennett glanced at her from the other side of the room. She was standing beside Brian, looking seriously irritated. Brian had a smirky smile on his face.

"Do you want lunch?" Frank demanded.

"Cory Potts from Mrs. Holden's class will lead us in the pledge..."

"Yes," Sammy hissed and tried to edge over to her table group.

"Pizza or..."

"I pledge allegiance...."

"...hamburger?"

"Frank!" Mrs. Bennett warned. Thankfully, Sammy put her hand over her heart and recited the pledge with the rest of the school. Mrs. Bennett insisted that all the students stand at attention during the pledge. Whatever Brian had done, plus the distraction of Frank would probably make her forget to send Sammy to the office.

"Mrs. Bennett," Frank called out as soon as the announcements were over, "doesn't Sammy have to go to the office? She came in way after the bell again."

"Only one minute!" Sammy turned a pleading

smile toward Mrs. Bennett.

Her teacher smiled wryly in return. "Be early tomorrow."

Sammy grinned. "I'll clean the boards for you," she promised.

"It's not fair," Frank sulked.

"Deal with it," Erin hissed at him.

Sammy smiled. "Sign me up for pizza, Frank."

During morning recess, Erin told everyone all about the dog. Marc and José perched on the edge of the bike rack. Lindsey, Celsa, and Chloe stood around. Sammy stood a few feet away, her back to them.

She could hear their sympathetic comments punctuating Erin's story, but she didn't want to talk about it. The whole thing was too important.

Instead she walked slowly across the asphalt yard. A fight was heating up by the basketball hoop. A couple of boys from the other sixth grade class were practicing shots. Brian had grabbed their ball. Laughing, he held it out of their reach as they complained loudly. The playground aide walked glumly toward them.

Sammy stood and watched. Brian bugged people almost every day.

"I just want to play too," Brian said in mock innocence. "It's a school ball. I should be able to play."

"You boys have to share," the aide said weakly.

"See!" Brian grinned.

"He took the ball!" one of the boys yelled in frustration. "He's wrecking the game."

"Do you boys want to go to the office and talk to the principal about this?"

"Yes!" the boy shouted. "It isn't fair! We don't want him!"

"Everybody always hurts my feelings," Brian said. "I don't want to play with you if you're going to be like that." He threw the ball way across the yard and stalked away leaving the two boys practically stamping in frustration.

Sammy watched him until he noticed her.

"What're you looking at?" he demanded.

"You." Sammy fished a package of Tic Tacs from her pocket and held them out. "Want one?"

His big hand closed around the box. Casually, he upended it into his mouth, letting a stream of mints rattle onto his tongue. Sammy gritted her teeth. It wasn't like she had the money to go buy candy every day. She took a deep breath. "I want to talk to you."

"Yeah? About what?" He handed back the nearly empty box.

"About Jack...your dog."

Brian's face hardened and he looked wary. "What about him?"

"Well...you want to sell him or something?"

"Maybe." Brian's eyes became calculating. "A hundred dollars."

"What! He's a mutt."

Brian smirked. "Yeah, but he's MY mutt. And if you want him, you'll have to pay for him."

"But where am I going to get a hundred dollars?" Sammy grabbed his arm. Brian shook her off easily.

"That's your problem." He walked away. A few feet from her he spat out the mouthful of Tic Tacs, laughed and never looked back.

40   Susan Brown

Chapter 4

Mind Your Own Business

Sammy laid her bike down on the grass behind Brian's yard and put a finger over her lips. Erin clapped a hand over an escaping giggle and dropped her bike down too.

"I feel like a thief," she whispered.

Sammy felt a lot more like a spy than a thief. If Brian's brothers knew she was there, she was sure they would do something to Jack, just to be mean. Careful not to make any sounds that would set the dog to barking, Sammy put her ear close to the vine-covered fence.

"Can you hear anything?" Erin whispered.

Sammy shook her head. "The coast is clear – I think."

Quickly she climbed the fence and hung over the top, scanning the yard. There was no sign of the boys. Jack was sitting at the end of his chain watching her. He didn't look friendly. In fact, as Sammy watched, his lip curled back into a soundless snarl.

Sammy felt the fence bounce as Erin climbed up beside her.

"What's going on?" she demanded. That was too much for Jack. The dog erupted into a barking frenzy, lunging against the chain, snarling and snapping.

"Easy boy, easy!" Sammy tried to soothe him. It was no use.

"Shut up, you dumb mutt!" The glass door into the house slid open and Joe strode out. The snarl on his face was crueler than the dog's. He was so intent on the barking animal he didn't look up.

Jack lowered his head and still barking backed behind the tree. Joe went after him.

"Stop!" Sammy shouted.

There was a sharp yelp, a whimper, and then silence. Sammy froze, feeling sick. An instant later Brian slammed outside. "Joe! I told you I was training Jack!" he shouted. "So just leave him alone!"

"And who's going to make me?" Joe demanded. He grabbed his brother's shirt, and slammed him against the tree trunk. Compared to the other sixth graders, Brian was huge. Compared to his brother, he was puny.

The dog started barking again, charging and retreating. A third time, the door opened and this time a middle-aged man, balding, bearded and short, strode into the yard. He wore tight jeans and a tighter T-shirt. With his open hand he slapped Joe.

"Knock it off," he ordered the boy. To Sammy's astonishment, Joe let go of his brother and stared sullenly down at the man.

"I wasn't doing nothin', Dad," he complained.

"Keep it that way," his father snapped back. He turned to the dog. "What's wrong with the pup? Quiet, you little devil."

Right on cue, Jack woofed and stared straight at the girls.

Sammy felt herself shrink a little as Mr. Haydon looked over. His eyebrows rose. "Can I help you two?"

That was all Erin needed. "We were checking on your dog, Mr. Haydon," she said. "Are you aware that your sons are abusing him?"

"It's illegal," Sammy told him. "You can get fined or arrested or...or worse!"

Mr. Haydon's expression didn't change. "How about you girls mind your own business," he said, "just like I mind mine. I could call your folks to complain about you trespassing on my property or I could call the police...or..." he grinned, "or worse."

Sammy knew she was beaten. Erin opened and then closed her mouth. Face burning, Sammy threw one look at the dog, and then dropped backwards off the fence. Erin followed. In the yard she heard the Haydons' voices and then the door slammed. She longed to climb up again, to look at Jack, but she was too scared. She yanked up her bike, so angry she didn't know whether to pound something or burst into tears.

"I can't believe he said that to us," Erin fumed. "He was wrong and he knew it."

"It is his property," Sammy muttered. But she knew that didn't matter. They were hurting Jack – and that was wrong.

But what was she going to do about it?

Sammy flipped through the channels a third time. Stupid – everything was really stupid. She left the channel on a commercial, shifted the book on her knee and tried to reread the chapter about the explorers. Her mom came into the room, picking at the bits of clay that hadn't washed from her fingernails.

"Anything on?" She sank down on the sofa beside her daughter.

Sammy shook her head. "Mom, would you loan me a hundred dollars?"

"What?"

"I'd pay it back or I'll work it off or do whatever you want, including keeping my room clean," Sammy said in a rush. "It's really important and I need it right now."

"Slow down," her mom commanded. She picked at another bit of pale grey clay. Sammy waited but her mom's attention seemed to have been lost already.

"This is serious, Mom!"

"What do you want a hundred dollars for?"

"The dog I told you about," Sammy said, trying to keep the impatience from her voice. "I told you about him before."

"Right. The dog that your friend has..."

"Brian is not my friend!"

Her mother gave her a look. "Sammy, I don't have a hundred dollars. And even if I did, I would not give it to you to buy a vicious dog that I don't want."

"I'd pay you back," Sammy's voice had dropped. "He's being hurt, Mom. I have to do something."

Her mom put her arm awkwardly around Sammy's shoulders. "Honey, it's not your responsibility. If you're really concerned, you can call the Humane Society...or I'll call them if you want."

"But you said they might destroy Jack," Sammy cried. "Because no one would want him. It isn't fair!" She pulled away from her mother and got up.

"Sammy!"

"I have to do my homework." She went into her room and threw herself on the bed. Papa Jack would have done something. But he wasn't there any more, so Sammy was the only one left to fix things. She reached for the pink bunny – the very last present Papa Jack had given her – and buried her face in its soft fur.

Like a photo being developed, the memory of Papa Jack giving it to her became clearer and clearer in her mind. It was Easter. She and her mom had hunted up all the candy eggs and piled them greedily in their baskets. Papa Jack had sat, avoiding extra movement in the antique rocker. His side hurt him so.

But he had held two parcels in his lap. A small one that he handed to Sammy's mother and a big crinkly one he handed to his granddaughter.

"I hope they're all right," he said. "I got them at the drugstore."

Sammy's Mom unwrapped her box. A crystal rabbit. She smiled and put it on the mantle. "It's great, Dad," she said and kissed him on the cheek.

Sammy pulled the paper off hers – it was a bunny too, but a large, pink plush one.

"Maybe you're too old for a pink bunny?" he had said.

"No! It's perfect," Sammy had declared, and buried her face in the soft fur. New smelling.

Sammy breathed deeply, now. The bunny still smelled new. A little. She rolled over, gazing up at the walls of her small bedroom. Ugly! Why did the renters pick such ugly colors? Maybe they were cheaper.

What should this color be called? Vomit yellow. If Papa Jack saw this color he would have taken her to the paint store right away. He would have helped her pick out something pretty – sky blue maybe.

She imagined how he would have shown her to stir the paint, dip the roller and then put the paint on the wall without splattering. That was how they'd done it two years ago when the tool shed needed painting.

Papa Jack had liked everything tidy. He wasn't like her friends' grandfathers. His black and grey hair was always combed; his mustache was always trimmed. Even when he got sick, when he could hardly walk across the room without panting because of the cancer in his ribs, he would shave and make sure his shirt matched his slacks.

Sammy squeezed the bunny to herself so hard, it hurt. She stared at the yellow wall, thinking how disgusting it was. But Papa Jack wouldn't have sat there feeling sorry for himself. He would have done something about it. Just like when the doctors said there were no treatments, he found a bunch of new ones, some even in other countries. He said they made him last longer. Not long enough. Sammy put aside the stuffed animal.

From the closet, Sammy hauled out the box of stuff brought from her room in the big house. First the kitten and fox posters, and then the postcards from Erin's trips, and the two yards of jungle material she'd intended to sew into a floor pillow. She dug deeper into the box and pulled out tacks. Then, from ceiling to floor, she started covering the walls.

Sammy didn't know what time it was when her mom came to the door. "Bed time, sweetie."

Flushed, Sammy shook her head. "I'm decorating."

Her mom took a few steps into the room and looked around. One wall was a checkerboard of posters and drawings torn from Sammy's biggest sketchpad. The window was framed in postcards. Sammy was battling the swath of jungle fabric, trying to get it pinned at an angle from the window.

"Eclectic," Linda announced.

"What?" Sammy twisted around from her perch on top of the desk, and the fabric dropped off the wall again.

"Eclectic – a mixture of styles. Want some help?"

Sammy hesitated, and then nodded. "I'm covering everything. It's...eclectic. You can put up anything, anywhere you want. Just no vomit yellow walls. None at all."

"Okay. You hold up the fabric. I'll pin."

In a moment the lions and elephants swept across the wall. Linda reached for a poster – a Dalmatian in a clutter of spotted white cats. It read: *In a world of copycats, be an original.* With a smile, she pinned it to the wall over Sammy's bed.

"What do you think?"

Sammy looked up. "Good. It looks good."

Her mom switched on the radio and handed Sammy a finely painted fan Papa Jack had brought back from a business trip. After that, they didn't talk except to ask for a tack or a poster or a picture. The hours crept by. Finally, the vomit yellow was gone. Draped fabric, posters, knick-knacks and drawings covered every inch.

Sammy sank down on her bed and gazed around.

Her mother kissed her on top of the head. "Now it's time for bed."

Too tired to say anything, Sammy slid down. She reached for the pink bunny; her eyes drifted shut. Then she felt the quilt being pulled around her and the warmth of it carrying her away.

The morning wasn't good. Sammy had forgotten all about washing her clothes again, so the cleanest shirt she had was spotty. The Cheerios lay in broken crumbs and dust in the bottom of the box. The milk had gone sour and she could hardly open her eyes.

"That's what happens when you stay up past two in the morning," her mother muttered over her coffee.

"That didn't make the milk turn sour," Sammy grumbled.

"Might have," her mom replied.

Sammy dumped the crumbs into a bowl, threw the box into the recycling bin and picked at the cereal with her fingers. "Can I buy lunch?"

"Not unless you pay for it yourself," her mom answered.

"I would if you ever gave me any money," Sammy snapped back. She was too tired to make a lunch and there was nothing left but one slice of ham anyway. Sammy searched through the fridge and then turned to the peanut butter jar. Empty. "A person could starve in this house."

"I left a piece of ham," her mom said. "And there are a couple of cookies left."

Exasperated, Sammy slapped the ham between two slices of bread, dropped it into a plastic container and threw in the two cookies. She looked longingly inside the fridge again. Nothing. In the old house, the fridge was always full. Papa Jack made a list every week and then went to the grocery store. Her mom didn't make lists. When she finally went to the store, she usually forgot a lot of stuff.

Sammy grabbed her backpack, jacket and meager lunch and headed out the door. Grimly, she pedaled up the hill away from the subdivision. She was going to be late. She had promised Mrs. Bennett she would be early, and she was going to be late anyway. Her face burned.

At the fence, she listened for any sounds. Nothing. Cautiously she toe-climbed up the fence. Jack stood watching her. Not friendly, but maybe not menacing either. His food dish was empty, but there was fresh water.

Her stomach growled. A half a bowl of cereal crumbs for breakfast. In her backpack, one piece of ham. Two slices of bread. Two cookies. Sammy sighed and took the meat from the bread.

"Here boy." She tossed the meat to Jack. It went down with one gulp. The pup seemed to dance on his toes. He pulled against the chain. Small whimpering noises slid from his throat. Sammy took a slice of bread and tossed it. Her aim wasn't so good, so Jack had to pull against the chain to reach it, but he seemed frantic. It was gone in a second. Sammy threw the last slice of bread. It disappeared too.

Jack looked up at her, brown eyes warm. Were they pleading?

"I only have two cookies left," Sammy told him.

The puppy watched and then he whimpered again. So low she could hardly hear him. She threw him the last cookies. Her stomach rumbled.

Chapter 5

A Really Bad Day

Sammy was so far away when school started that the bell sounded like an echo floating over the hills. She bit her lip and pumped harder. The wind felt chilly all of a sudden and the clouds started spitting at her.

The road was slick and slippery by the time she wheeled into the schoolyard. This time she didn't even try to sneak into the classroom. Mrs. Bennett was nice, but not that nice. The pledge was already over when she got to the office. Mrs. Pope, the office manager, looked up from her computer.

"Late again, Sammy?"

Sammy nodded, too out of breath to talk. Mrs. Pope brought her the sign-in book and marked the time: *9:12*.

"You need to get up earlier," she told Sammy. "Don't you have an alarm clock?"

Sammy awkwardly signed her name. "I slept through it."

"Well, maybe you need to go to bed a little earlier. What do you think?"

Sammy tried to smile. "I suppose so. I was decorating my room last night...and it got really late."

Mrs. Pope took back the sign-in book and handed her an *Admit To Class* slip. "This is your third tardy this month. Ms. Martinez will probably call your mother."

Sammy sighed. "I know. Thanks, Mrs. Pope." As she turned to go, her stomach rumbled loudly.

"Was that you? Did you eat breakfast this morning?"

Sammy felt her face heat up. "I...um...I was in such a rush...trying to get here on time."

"Well, you need some breakfast." She opened one of her cupboards and took out a giant sized box of granola bars. "Apple cinnamon or raisin?"

"Apple cinnamon, please." Sammy took it gratefully. "Should I go to my class now?"

"No, you sit down here on the bench and eat. A couple of minutes more won't matter." She smiled, went into the principal's office, and closed the door.

Sammy ate the bar, licked her fingers and feeling much more cheerful, went to her classroom. Mrs. Bennett had already started the math lesson. The tables were spread with pattern blocks and she had the overhead projector turned on with pattern block shapes spread across it. Sammy gave her the admit slip and received a packet of papers in return.

"Okay everybody, let's try the first three problems."

Sammy waved at Erin, two tables over, and slid into her own chair. She looked over at Tara's and John Markus' paper. "What are we doing?" she whispered.

"You put the pattern blocks on the diagrams on the paper," Tara said, "and then you figure out what the fraction is."

"It's really easy," John Markus told her.

The first three problems were easy. After that it got harder as the pieces and the fractions had to be added up. Tara was working quickly, humming to herself. John Markus seemed okay too, except they'd written down different answers. Sammy couldn't get her mind on it. Who cared how many little green triangles made a yellow hexagon? She glanced around the room to see what her other friends were doing.

Erin was giggling with Jordan. Chloe and Isabella were trying out different combinations of the green triangles, red trapezoids and blue rhombuses. Behind and to the right of her,

Brian sat slouched over his desk, his face in his hands. Sammy could just see the edges of a swelling purple bruise on his cheek. She winced. Looked like Joe had gotten him after all.

She bit her lip. Was it her fault, because she had started the dog barking? Her stomach turned at the memory of Joe slamming Brian against the tree and the sound of his Dad's slap.

About the time they were on problem six, the principal, Ms. Martinez, glided in.

"Could I borrow Brian for a couple of minutes, Mrs. Bennett," she said. Her voice always sounded sweet and silvery to Sammy.

"Of course." Mrs. Bennett smiled.

"What'd I do?" Brian demanded suspiciously.

"Nothing. I just need your help for a few minutes." Ms. Martinez smiled again.

That clinched it, Sammy thought. If you were in trouble, Mrs. Pope called you down to the office over the PA. Then you sat on the bench and waited until Ms. Martinez was ready to talk to you.

But if the principal came to get you, the trouble was the quiet, scary kind. Sammy fingered a blue pattern piece. Mrs. Bennett must have spotted Brian's bruises and told the office. Everybody knew that Kyle and Joe had hit Brian before. Was it her fault this time?

The rest of the period dragged.

When the bell rang for first recess, Erin made a beeline for her. "How come you were so late?"

Sammy shrugged. "I slept in."

"I bet they're going to call your mother!" Erin smiled and her white teeth flashed. "And then you'll be seriously grounded."

Sammy shook her head. "My mother says grounding me is too much work because she has to make sure I stay in my room. She'll probably just yell."

"My mother never yells," Erin said. "She goes for major guilt."

"You two are so lucky." Lindsey pulled a brush through her long hair and then expertly twisted it into a ponytail. "I get grounded for weeks."

Mrs. Bennett came over then and shooed them outside. "But it's raining," Lindsey tried. "You wouldn't send us out in the rain, would you?"

"Just like that!" Mrs. Bennett snapped her fingers, smiled and held the door open.

"I could clean the boards for you now," Sammy offered.

Mrs. Bennett shook her head. "Later."

The kids filed out. On the playground Sammy looked around for Brian. There was no sign of him. She slouched against the brick wall. Erin leaned against the wall beside her.

"Did you really sleep in?" she asked. "Or was it the dog?"

"It was Jack," Sammy said. "I fed him my lunch."

"It's lucky for you Mom thinks I don't eat enough," Erin said. "I've got loads."

"Good, thanks." Sammy stared out at the kids playing basketball. "Did you see Brian's face?"

"Uh huh. His brother must've really beat on him. What a loser." Erin's mouth pinched up in disgust.

"Do you...do you think it was our fault for being there?" Sammy asked. "I mean, we started Jack barking and everything."

Erin's head tilted to one side as she thought about it. "Well, I made the dog bark, not you. But there's no way Brian's black eye is our fault. I mean, my brothers fight all the time and they never really hurt each other – at least not on purpose."

Sammy nodded gratefully. "Yeah, you're right. They're just a bunch of losers."

Brian reappeared in class after recess during silent reading. His face was hot red except for a swollen bruise across his cheek.

Without looking at anyone, he opened a book and stared at it. Mrs. Bennett said nothing, but gave him an extra wide smile. Considering that he always fooled around during silent reading and the rest of the time made Mrs. Bennett crazy, whatever happened must've been a big deal. Sammy glanced over to see if Erin had noticed, but her friend was buried in her book. Sammy looked back at Brian.

"What're you looking at," he growled.

"Nothing," she whispered. "Your face... does it hurt?"

Brian shook his head and glued his eyes back on the book.

"Sammy, this is silent reading," Mrs. Bennett reminded her.

The rest of the morning was okay, except that Sammy began to get sleepier and sleepier. At lunchtime, Mrs. Martinez wandered into the lunchroom and sat at their table for a while. When she saw Erin sharing her lunch with Sammy, she shared hers too, and then everybody at the table made a pile of their food like a picnic. That was fun. Mrs. Martinez looked really young for a principal and giggled when someone made a joke. Sammy liked the way she giggled.

A few minutes later the principal went to sit at some of the other tables.

Sammy propped her head on her hands and sleepily watched the kids dump their leftovers into the trash can. At least half the kids didn't eat more than a couple of bites of their sandwiches. What a waste.

When Erin had to go to the bathroom, Sammy lingered by the garbage can and cautiously checked it out. Some of the sandwiches hadn't even been unwrapped. With this stuff, she could keep Jack fed for days.

She reached in, grabbed a wrapped bagel and cream cheese in one hand and what looked like a tuna sandwich in the other. That's when she saw Mrs. Martinez.

"Sammy," the principal said quietly, "what are you doing?"

"I...uh...I," Sammy felt herself start to burn up. There wasn't a hint of laughter in Ms. Martinez' voice now. Brian came up behind and started to empty his tray.

"Sammy?" Ms. Martinez repeated.

Sammy's eyes slid to Brian's bruised face. "I...um...it's these sandwiches... they're perfectly good. See? Not even opened. And I...um...can't stand to see them just thrown away...you know, waste not want not..." Sammy was babbling and she knew it. Brian stared at her as though she'd lost her mind. "...and I thought they'd make a good snack...for after school...or something..."

Ms. Martinez took the sandwiches from her hands and dropped them into the trash. "I don't think that's a very sanitary snack," she said. "Why don't you come down to my office and we'll talk about it."

"I'd rather not," Sammy protested. "And besides, I don't want to miss any more school... after being late..."

"It won't take long," the principal said.

Miserably, Sammy trailed along behind her to the office. She had almost made up her mind to tell Ms. Martinez the truth when she saw Brian's father standing awkwardly near Mrs. Pope's desk.

"Mr. Haydon is here to see you," Mrs. Pope told the principal.

Ms. Martinez smiled and held out her hand. "Thank you for coming, Mr. Haydon." They shook hands. Sammy shrank back when Brian's father glanced at her, but there was no recognition. "I have to look after a couple of things," the principal went on. "Would you mind waiting just a few minutes? It won't take long. And I'd like our counselor, Mrs. Sovich to be here too."

Mr. Haydon nodded his consent and Ms. Martinez led Sammy into her office. She pointed to a chair for Sammy, made a couple of notes on a yellow pad of paper, then sat down beside her.

"So Sammy, what's going on?" the principal asked.

"Nothing."

"That's not what I've been noticing." She waited and when Sammy kept silent, she started ticking off her fingers. "You were late this morning for the third time in a week and a half; the day before yesterday, you got in a fight with four other girls; today, Mrs. Pope gave you breakfast; Erin shared her lunch with you because you didn't seem to have one; then you were going through the garbage for leftover sandwiches. That doesn't seem like nothing to me."

"It won't happen again," Sammy pleaded. "It's just been a really bad day. You wouldn't believe how bad it's been."

"Can you tell me about it?"

Sammy wanted to bury her face in her hands. She wanted to tell Ms. Martinez everything about her mother and Papa Jack and the dog – but Mr. Haydon was standing just outside the door.

"There's nothing to tell...I just didn't get enough sleep and I forgot to make my lunch, that's all."

Ms. Martinez looked at her intently for a moment. Sammy lifted her chin and stared back. Ms. Martinez tapped a finger on the table, then said, "Okay, but if you do have something you'd like to talk about, tell your teacher or me or Mrs. Pope. Okay?"

"Okay." Sammy stood up gratefully.

"I'm going to call your mother again and try to set up a conference," Ms. Martinez said. "It's school policy for all those tardies." She scribbled a note on a pad of *Admit To Class* slips and handed it to Sammy. "Go on back to class now."

Sammy ducked her head as she passed Mr. Haydon, but he didn't notice her. When she came back to the room, Mrs. Bennett had just started a science video about atoms. The kids were sitting on the floor in front of the screen. Sammy dropped her admit slip on Mrs. Bennett's desk and then edged in beside Erin.

With the sound of the video masking her, Erin whispered, "What happened?"

Sammy glanced at Brian. He was out of earshot. "I was getting sandwiches from the trash to feed Jack, and Ms. Martinez saw me. She thinks I wanted them for myself!"

"Why?" Erin demanded.

Sammy began to giggle. "Because I told her I did. She thinks I'm the school's first bag lady!"

Erin giggled too, and then a thought struck her. "Will she call your Mom?"

Sammy stopped laughing abruptly. "I'm dead."

Chapter 6

A Girl Who Wants to Work

When the end of the day bell finally rang, Sammy made good her promise to clean the boards. But instead of taking the time to chat with Mrs. Bennett, she swiped the cloth fast across the white board, and then raced for her bike.

With her helmet jammed on her head, Sammy tore down the street toward the Haydon's house – toward Jack. She wheeled up, hopped off and dropped her bike on the grassy curb.

And then she stopped.

If she climbed the fence, Jack might bark. Maybe Joe would come out and hit him. She had no food for the puppy. She would only get him hurt again.

Sammy sank down beside her bike, wrapped her arms around her knees and tucked her heels tight against the curb. The sensible thing would be to go home – but she couldn't. When

Papa Jack lay dying, the nurses had made her and her mom go home to sleep. You can't do anything, they said. But it hurt so bad to leave him there alone.

Sammy got on her bike and pedaled toward the business district.

A hundred dollars. Brian wanted a hundred dollars for his pup. How could she earn that much money? Baby-sitting? No one had ever asked her. Maybe she could put out fliers.

Sammy steered into the parking lot of the convenience store. She was dying of thirst and didn't even have the money for a can of pop. Balancing on her bike, she stared at the door. A sign in the window read *Help Wanted*.

She shoved her bike in the rack, pushed back her tangled hair and walked in.

The store was like every other convenience store. There were racks of snack food, a wall-size cooler full of milk, pop and beer, and the air smelled of the greasy food kept hot under red lights. A tall old man, stooped and pot-bellied with sticky grey hair, watched her from watery blue eyes. Sammy walked up to the counter.

"The sign says you need help," she said.

The old man simply stared without changing expression.

"Can I...I want...I mean...I um, need a job." Sammy felt her face heat up hotter and hotter.

A shadow of a smile crossed the old man's face. It disappeared so fast Sammy thought it must have been a twitch. Then he turned to the freezee machine, filled a small cup, then slid it across the counter to Sammy.

"No, I don't have any money." She put her hands behind her back. "I want a job."

"It's a hot day." The voice was deep and splintery, like it wasn't used often. "Take it. I'm looking for a nighttime cashier. But kids, they don't want to work for low pay. Nobody but us old folks. I think a girl who wants to work needs a drink on a hot day."

He turned away and began slowly filling a cigarette rack from a box behind the counter. Sammy hesitated then took the freezee.

"Thank you!" she called as she went out the door. The old man seemed to grunt a reply, but maybe it was just the effort of bending down.

The sun was setting and the shadows on the road were getting darker. Sammy stopped by yet another curb and squinted her eyes down the street, into the sun. She had tried every store she could think of – Safeway, Payless, and a whole lot of little stores. Some of the managers had been really nice, a couple had been annoyed. But the answer had been the same at all of them: they didn't hire anyone younger than sixteen.

Ahead were a series of one-story office type buildings.

"This is so stupid," Sammy said aloud. She jumped back as a car whizzed by and its horn blared. Determined, she pushed off again. Papa Jack had said the only losers were quitters. She wasn't a quitter.

Another car sped by. Sammy turned into a long circular drive, away from the rush hour traffic. Ahead was a well-lit entrance to the building. *McCracken Senior Care,* the scrolled white sign read.

A few raindrops splattered down. Sammy sighed. Now she would get soaked as well. She leaned her bike against a square pillar and jogged to the entrance.

The lobby walls shone a muted sterile white, broken by an artificial plant in one corner. Sammy did a quick check – empty except for a grey-haired woman slumped on a sofa and a receptionist busily sorting mail at a long counter. She didn't take her worried eyes off the woman, even when Sammy walked in the door.

"Excuse me..." Sammy's voice echoed sharply in the lobby. She blushed and dropped the volume. "Excuse me..."

The receptionist shifted her attention. "Can I help you?"

Sammy took a deep breath. "I hope so. My name is Sammy...Samantha Connor. I'm looking for a part-time job. I'll do just about anything...and I learn fast."

She smiled hopefully.

"I'm sorry, sweetie. But we..." She stopped abruptly, tapped the edge of a letter on her teeth and glanced at the woman on the sofa. "I don't know, honey...Can you read?"

"Yes," Sammy said indignantly.

The receptionist smiled. "I mean can you read really well...something like this." She came from behind the counter, picked up a magazine and handed it to Sammy. "Here, read the first article."

Sammy felt her face heat up. The woman on the sofa lifted her head and stared at her intently. Sammy thumbed to the right page, took a shaky breath, and started at the top.

There were only a few hard words. Sammy guessed at them well enough that the receptionist didn't notice.

"Very nice, honey," the receptionist interrupted after a couple of paragraphs. She turned to the other woman. "What do you think, Mrs. La Mantea?"

"I'm ready to try anything." Mrs. La Mantea came over and looked at Sammy closely. "I've had to bring my mother here. She had a stroke...and I can't..." the woman's eyes filled with tears.

"I know. It's hard." The receptionist patted Mrs. La Mantea's shoulder. "But, you know it's for the best."

"I suppose. But she's so lonely and I can't get here more than once or twice a week. Mom's eyes are affected and she loves books so much. Would you be willing to read to her for an hour a day? I could pay you five dollars?"

Five dollars! Quickly, Sammy did the math in her head. Twenty-five a week...

"What about weekends?" Sammy asked.

"Oh, I can come then. Even a half an hour a day would be all right, but it would have to be every day."

"I'll do it," Sammy said quickly. She'd have the money in a month. "What if I read longer than an hour?"

Mrs. La Mantea suddenly looked a little suspicious. "Probably the hour will be enough. The nurse will keep track of your hours for me."

Sammy felt herself flush. "I won't cheat you."

"Of course not," the woman said quickly. "Come and meet mother. This is a godsend. And mother is so fond of children..."

Sammy followed her down a long corridor to the left. The floor was a smooth beige carpet, the walls a dull green. Every ten feet or so, a door opened off the corridor. Mrs. La Mantea went in the third one on the right. The sign on the door read, *Mrs. Betancourt*.

Inside, Sammy saw an old woman lying against several pillows in a tilted up bed. Some of her dark grey hair had pulled out of a twisted bun and spread in untidy ripples on the pillowcase. Her face was wide and creased like white crepe paper that had yellowed in the sun. The right side of her face looked saggy, as though it were made of dough, not flesh. Her right arm lay motionless at her side. Even though her eyelids were closed, she plucked again and again at the edge of the sheet with her left hand.

"Mom," Mrs. La Mantea said. "I've brought someone to meet you."

The woman didn't open her eyes, but her fingers stopped moving and her head rolled away from them.

Mrs. La Mantea's eyes got watery again. "This may not work," she said.

"Yes it will," Sammy blurted out. She had to have this job. She couldn't lose it now. Sammy walked over to the bed. "Mrs. Betancourt," she said loudly. "I'm Sammy Connor. I'm going to read to you. I can start right now if you'd like."

The grey head rolled back. The heavy eyelids opened, the left wider than the right, but both showed steely grey eyes.

Sammy lifted her chin. "I'm a good reader. I'll come every day, rain or shine. I promise."

"What does a girl like you want to be reading to an old woman like me for?" Her voice was heavy and slurry, like her tongue was too big.

"Your daughter is paying me. I need the money to buy something special."

"What? A TV? A computer game? Teenage things."

Sammy felt slightly flattered at being mistaken for a teenager. "No. It's for something important."

The old woman's eyes narrowed. "What?"

Sammy met her look. "Do you want me to read to you tonight?"

The woman shut her eyes again. Sammy wanted to shake her. She sure didn't seem like someone who liked kids.

"Tomorrow." Her lips hardly seemed to move. "I want you to read a book of poetry to me. Robert Frost and Browning and Dylan

Thomas." Her eyes opened. "You don't even know who they are, do you?"

"No." Sammy shook her head. "I'll go to the library and find them though."

"Do that," the old woman's voice rumbled like distant thunder, and she shut her eyes again. Sammy watched as her creased mouth drifted open and her breathing became more soft thunder.

They tiptoed out. Mrs. La Mantea seemed ready to cry again. The receptionist looked very pleased with herself.

"I think it will be okay," Mrs. La Mantea said to the receptionist. "Don't you?"

The other woman answered with a smile. Mrs. La Mantea kept talking all the way to the front lobby, not waiting for an answer from anyone. Sammy recited in her head: Frost, Browning and Dylan Thomas...Frost, Browning and Dylan Thomas.

They would pay for Jack.

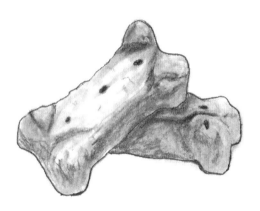

Chapter 7

I'll Make You Sorry

The clock on the principal's desk clicked to 9:48 a.m. Mrs. Sovich, the counselor, had come and gone, but Sammy, her mother, and the principal were still sitting around the table with the bowl of candy in the center. No one had taken any.

Sammy noticed that her mother's neck was bright red and the color was slowly creeping up her jawline. Despite that, her mother smiled again at the principal.

"I don't really understand why Sammy has been late so often, Mrs. Martinez," she repeated. "I wake her up every morning in plenty of time, and we always have breakfast together." She swiveled toward Sammy. "Isn't that right, Samantha?"

Sammy twisted wet fingers in her lap. Her mother never called her Samantha. The red flush was up to her mom's cheekbones now, and it scared Sammy.

"Yes," she said. Her voice sounded so strange to her own ears, that she repeated, "Yes," more loudly.

"Sammy didn't have any lunch yesterday," Mrs. Martinez went on. "And later she was taking other students' lunches from the trash. She said it was for a snack later."

Linda Connor's eyes widened. "Sammy!" Her voice had lost all her uncertainty. "What are you trying to pull?"

"Nothing," Sammy defended herself. "They were perfectly good sandwiches – they hadn't even been unwrapped. And Papa Jack always said, 'Waste not, want not' and it was a waste, so I was taking them for later. I mean, why throw away perfectly good food? There are children starving somewhere, aren't there?"

"I don't understand this." Linda Connor turned to the principal. "I've explained that Sammy's been having a very hard time with her grandfather's death and I suppose she's acting out."

Mrs. Martinez said nothing. She watched them both.

"I'm not acting out," Sammy muttered. "And I'm still in the room so you don't have to talk about me as if I wasn't here." She and her mother glared at each other.

"Sammy," her mother said coldly. "Please behave yourself."

That did it. Sammy felt the firecrackers exploding in her head again – loud, red ones with screamers. She leapt up from her chair. "What do you care how I behave? You don't bother with me anyway. You never bother with anything you don't want to!"

"Sammy! Stop it!" her mother snapped. "You know that isn't true!"

"Oh yeah!" Sammy shouted. "I was starving because you don't like to go shopping so there was nothing to eat except a slice of ham and the cookies I made. And you don't give me any money to buy anything with so what am I supposed to do? You don't care about anything but yourself. You didn't even care that Papa Jack died and he's your father!"

Her mother's face had gone dead white. "Sammy, I'm warning you...stop it!"

Sammy slapped her hands over her mouth. Mrs. Martinez stood up, put an arm around her shoulders and a firm hand on her arm. "Sammy, that's enough. You're very angry but we can work this out without shouting at each other. Can't we?"

Sammy stole a look at her mother. Her mom was sitting with her hands curled into fists in her lap and her back as straight as a yardstick. She was staring at the wall.

"I'm sorry, Mom." Sammy whispered.

Her mother nodded. "We'll talk later. I'll see you after school." She got up and started toward the door. Then abruptly she pivoted, looked resentfully at the principal and leaned over to give Sammy a quick kiss on the cheek. "Later."

"You were gone forever," Erin probed at recess. "What happened? Are you grounded?"

Sammy shook her head. She didn't want to talk about it. After her mom left, Sammy sat in the corner of a big chair trying to stop crying while Mrs. Martinez worked. When the recess bell rang, she told the principal she was all right. Mrs. Martinez let her go, but told Sammy she had to have lunch with the school counselor.

"Erin," she said. "I need a huge favor."

"What?" Erin looked interested.

"I need your lunch."

"The whole thing?"

Sammy nodded. "I fed Jack my lunch again this morning. And I told Mrs. Martinez that my mother doesn't buy me any food and she says I have to have lunch with Mrs. Sovich, the counselor, and if I show up without any lunch again, they'll think my mother is starving me or something. I'm desperate."

Erin shook her head. "You aren't desperate; you're dead. Your mother is going to kill you."

"I know," Sammy groaned. "She said we'd talk after school."

"Uh oh."

"I need a lunch," Sammy pleaded.

Erin giggled. "You owe me for this, Sammy Connor. They're having gross-out corn dogs for lunch and my mother packed me a Twinkie."

"I'll save it for you."

Erin shook her head. Her black hair shone like silk in the sun. "Enjoy. I think I'm gaining weight anyway."

"No way. You're so thin."

They started wandering around the schoolyard, watching other kids. Sammy told Erin about her job reading to old Mrs. Betancourt. "If I read every day, I'll have enough money for Jack in a month."

"Wow," Erin said. "That's really good. Is your Mom happy?"

Sammy felt herself heat up. "I didn't tell her. When I finally got home last night, she'd gone to another art class at the community college. She thought I was at your house, so she just left me some mac and cheese."

"Oh," Erin said.

"I didn't want to face her last night anyway," Sammy insisted. "Look. There's Brian. I'm going to tell him about my job." She took off before Erin could say anything more.

For once, Brian wasn't bugging anyone. He had a long stick and was drawing angry sweeps and squiggles in the dirt, then scratching them out.

"Hi!" Sammy said. Brian didn't even look up. "Your face looks better. Does it hurt?"

Brian shook his head. "Not much."

"Did Kyle and Joe do it?"

He nodded. "I hate my brothers. I hate my Dad too. I'm going to run away to live with my Mom." He went on drawing in the dirt.

"Where is she?"

"San Francisco. That's where her Christmas card came from last year. She didn't put on a return address, but I can find her."

Scratch, scratch, sweep it out. "They beat on me all the time...especially now that...."

Sammy hunched over and shoved her hands in her jeans pockets. "Now that what?"

Brian shook his head and went on scratching through the dirt. "Mrs. Martinez, she calls CPS and that social worker doesn't do nothin' but talk. Dad makes Joe and Kyle stop when he's around, but he works nights.

He doesn't have a clue." Brian raised his head and looked up across the subdivision that surrounded the school. "I'm going to run away to San Francisco. And if you tell anyone, I'll make you sorry."

"I won't tell. But you won't leave Jack with your brothers, will you?" Sammy begged. "I found a job. I'll earn a hundred in a month. Don't leave Jack with your brothers, please, Brian."

He shrugged. "Jack was a nice puppy. If I can get money together, I'm out of here. But I'll bring him to you, and you can give me what you got."

"Deal!" Sammy declared. The recess bell rang, so she spun and jogged toward the door.

"You'll still owe me," Brian called after her. He threw the stick high, watched it whirl around and around, until it dropped over the fence into someone's garden. Then, taking his time, he started toward the school door.

The rest of the morning crept along. Mrs. Bennett was into grammar today. Too many kids had made dumb mistakes on the last assignment and so she was determined to teach everybody everything before lunch.

Sammy sighed and finished copying the paragraph from the board. Mrs. Bennett said it had about 35 mistakes in it. Sammy figured if she found half it would be okay. She propped her head on her fist and surreptitiously watched Brian. He was drawing cartoons on his paper. Mrs. Bennett was pretending she hadn't noticed yet. Erin was squinting at the board and then rapidly writing down corrections. Sammy bet she'd get them all. Erin loved that stuff.

It occurred to Sammy that Brian might not know her phone number. What if he left and forgot about Jack? In a swell of panic, Sammy tore off the bottom of the page and scribbled:

I live at 1 Connor Lane (the old white painted place back of the trees). My number is 360-644-9710. DON'T FORGET TO CALL ME!!! I don't care when.
Sammy
(P.S. I'll have the money waiting)

She leaned back, pretended to stretch and dropped the note on Brian's desk. He didn't notice. Mrs. Bennett, however, did.

"I think you dropped this." She scooped the note off the desk and handed it back to Sammy. "Finish your paragraph, please." She turned to Brian. "Either you finish this Brian, or you do it at recess. Frankly, I don't care which."

Brian smirked, picked up his paper and began folding it into an airplane. "I'll do it at recess."

"Yeah, right," Frank chimed in. "Mrs. Bennett, he has to see Mrs. Martinez at recess. He told me so this morning before school."

Sammy crouched over her paper, note crumpled inside her fist, ignoring the confrontation between Brian and their teacher. Later, at lunch recess, she'd have to get the note to him – if he ever got out of the principal's office. She sighed, remembering the counselor – if she ever got out either.

84   Susan Brown

Chapter 8

No Problem

"So I hear things haven't been going so well?" Mrs. Sovich, the counselor, set a can of root beer on the table in front of Sammy and a Diet Coke at her own place. She sat down and opened a container of salad. Taking the cue, Sammy opened Erin's lunch sack. She was careful to keep Erin's name turned away from the counselor.

"Do you want to tell me what's going on?" Mrs. Sovich asked.

Sammy thought about saying "No," then leaving. Somehow she didn't think even Brian would have the nerve for that.

"There isn't a lot going on," Sammy said. "My grandfather died during the summer and my mother is having trouble coping. That's all." She eyed the counselor under her lashes. "I think she's acting out."

Sammy smiled when the counselor choked back a laugh.

"Very good," Mrs. Sovich said. "But I think there's more to it than that. And whatever it is, it's affecting your work here, so we need to deal with it."

Sammy clenched her teeth. There was no way she was going to tell anyone about anything.

But Mrs. Sovich kept asking questions and she didn't seem to care when it wasn't any of her business. Sammy found herself talking a lot about how her mother hardly ever went shopping. Like that was what really mattered.

"You're feeling a little neglected then?" the counselor probed.

Sammy had had enough. "No," she said. "I'm feeling like my grandfather died. I want him back and I can't have him." She stood up, slamming back the chair. But she spoiled the effect by realizing part way out the office door that she had forgotten Erin's lunch sack.

She hesitated just long enough for Mrs. Sovich to call after her, "I'll see you at lunch again tomorrow."

Sammy kept going.

Brian was let out of Mrs. Martinez' office at the same time. They headed toward the playground without acknowledging each other. When they passed from the cool shadow of the hallway to the outside glare of the asphalt, they both relaxed.

"Man, I wish she'd stop using up my recess," Brian said. "It's getting really old."

Sammy perched on the edge of the bike rack. "I've got to go back tomorrow."

"Me too." Brian gazed across the tarmac at a group of third graders hurling a basketball at the rusty hoop. He leaned against the wall. "If I get another warning slip, I get suspended."

"So?" Sammy challenged him. "You don't like school anyway. What's so bad about a three day vacation?"

Brian didn't answer, just glowered at the kids on the court. Sammy fished the note she'd written earlier from her pocket and thrust it into Brian's hand.

"Here," she said. "This is my address and phone number. Just in case."

Before Brian could reply, Sammy jumped down from the bike rack. She'd better find Erin. They had to get the lunch sack back before Mrs. Sovich noticed Erin's name on the front.

But the bell rang, just as Sammy spotted her strolling around the playground with Jordan and Lily. They had returned to the classroom and gotten out their books for silent reading before Sammy could tell Erin that she'd left the lunch sack in Mrs. Sovich's office.

"Can't I just get it after school?" Erin whispered.

Sammy darted a glance at Mrs. Bennett. She was busy loading a new program on the computers. "No," Sammy hissed. "If you get the lunch sack, they'll know I didn't have one and my mother will really kill me."

"But I don't want to lie," Erin said unhappily.

"What lie?" Sammy demanded. "I just want you to cover for me if Mrs. Bennett asks where I am."

"But if I tell her you've gone to the bathroom while you're in the office, that's a lie."

Sammy rubbed her nose. "Okay, so I'll go to the bathroom on my way to the office."

Erin nodded, pleased. "No problem." She turned her attention back to her book.

Sammy wanted to giggle and she wasn't quite sure why. Maybe it was the craziness of the whole thing. Maybe it was because these days she felt like somebody else half the time.

Brian had given her the idea of how to get the lunch sack. As she chose a new book from the shelf, a prickly feeling on the back of her neck made her look up.

It was like a twisted version of her dream about Papa Jack. Instead of the puppy looking in the window, Joe and Kyle, Brian's brothers, stood there. They were black silhouettes with the sun behind, but Sammy could easily see their gesture to Brian, ordering him outside. Brian had shaken his head. The menacing look they gave him made her shiver. They didn't even gesture again – just fixed him with their snake eyes. Brian's cheeks flushed and he bit his lip. Like a puppet, he got up, slipped his card into the restroom slot and disappeared into the hallway.

Ten minutes had passed. Fifteen. Through the open classroom door, she saw Mrs. Sovich and Ms. Martinez walking down the hall together toward the primary classrooms. If Sammy left now, supposedly to go to the bathroom, they wouldn't be in their offices. They wouldn't see that the lunch bag wasn't hers – they wouldn't ask any more questions.

But Brian had put his card in the only restroom slot. Sammy would have risk breaking the rule about leaving the room.

She slipped out of her chair, and walked casually over to the wall chart by the door. Pretending to be surprised at Brian's card in the slot, she glanced over her shoulder. Mrs. Bennett was still staring at the screen and typing. So far, so good. Sammy left the room.

All down the hall she could hear the murmur of kids' voices overlaid with louder teacher voices. No one but a little kid, happily singing off-key on his way back from the bathroom was in the corridor.

Sammy pushed into the girl's bathroom. Empty. She waited to the count of ten, turned around and walked out again. There. Erin didn't have to tell a lie.

"This is no big deal at all," Sammy said aloud.

Getting the lunch sack was easy. Mrs. Pope was on the phone. The counselor's door was open. When the office manager looked up, Sammy smiled her "good kid" smile and sailed into the office. Erin's bag was where she'd left it on the table. Letting out her breath, she grabbed the lunch sack and waved to Mrs. Pope on her way out. Simple. No problem.

The playground door was to the left of the office. Through the wavy glass, she could make out three figures. Brian and his brothers.

Sammy shook her head. "If you get caught, Brian, Mrs. Martinez is going to kill you," she said softly.

That's when it happened. Joe grabbed Brian's shirt in both hands and shoved him hard against the brick wall. Kyle crowded in, fist cocked. Even through the thick door, Sammy heard Brian's cry.

"Stop it!" she yelled. If they heard her, they didn't care. Kyle's fist was circling, getting closer and closer to Brian's face.

Sammy spun on her heel and ran back into the office.

"Mrs. Pope! Mrs. Pope, they're hurting him!" she cried. "You've got to come. You've got to make them stop!"

The office manager looked up, startled. She looked at the phone, then hurriedly said into the receiver, "I'll have to get back to you."

She hurried around the desk and into the hall with Sammy. Nothing. The glass was empty. They were gone.

"Sammy, what happened?"

"Brian's brothers came. He sneaked out of class and was talking to them outside. But they were hitting him!"

The office manager's lips tightened fiercely. "Go get Mrs. Martinez. She's in Mrs. Holden's room."

Mrs. Pope strode out the doors, calling towards the playground. "Hey there! Brian!"

Sammy sped down the hall toward Mrs. Holden's room. Mrs. Martinez was sitting at a table with some kids, listening to a story one had written.

"Mrs. Martinez! Mrs. Pope needs you. Right away!" Sammy blurted out.

Mrs. Martinez' eyes widened. She smiled at the boy who had been reading, murmured, "That was great, Matt," and disappeared from the room.

Sammy just stood there, not knowing what to do. Mrs. Holden solved the problem for her.

"Now that you've delivered your message, Sammy," the teacher said calmly. "You'd better go back to class."

Out in the hallway, Sammy hesitated. Turning on her heel, she walked past the office door craning to see in. Empty.

Should she wait around to see what happened, go back to class, or check the playground for Brian? What if Brian's brothers came after her? But what if Brian needed help?

"This is so dumb," she said under her breath. Keeping an eye out for the adults, Sammy pushed the door open and headed for the playground. Empty. Being careful to keep away from any classroom windows, she jogged to the playing field. There was a stand of trees that would hide the boys from view.

It was a long way from the school. If someone (like herself) yelled for help, no one would hear. Sammy's breath came hard. If the boys were there, maybe shouting from a distance would make them stop.

She squinted, trying to distinguish between the bright sun and flashing shadows. Empty. No one was there. She trotted back toward the school, wondering if she should go through the parking lot and check the road. No. Mrs. Pope was already there, looking up and down the street. Mrs. Martinez was nowhere to be seen.

When Mrs. Pope started slowly back toward the school, Sammy gave it up. With relief, she darted inside.

Instead of going to class, she went to the bathroom again. For several minutes, she washed her face and hands, and then she fussed with her hair (like she could make any difference). When a couple of second grade girls barreled in, she left.

Once again, she cruised past the office. Lips tight, Mrs. Pope was banging hard on her keyboard. Mrs. Martinez' door was shut. For once, Sammy hoped Brian was in there with her.

He wasn't in the classroom. Sammy silently stashed the lunch sack on the shelf by the door and slipped into her seat. The teacher barely glanced her way.

Erin leaned over and whispered. "I told Mrs. Bennett that you'd gone to the bathroom. That you couldn't wait. But what took so long?"

"I'll tell you later." Sammy picked up her book. Her hands were shaking.

Chapter 9

Miles to Go

Carefully, Erin parted the leaves and flowers of the vine woven through the chain-link fence. Once she'd cleared a peep-hole, she pressed her eye to the spot.

"The coast is clear," she whispered. "Nobody in the yard. No lights in the house."

Sammy nodded. Where was Brian? she wondered. Well, Jack was her first priority.

When she topped the fence, Jack was waiting. He sat there, at the end of his chain watching her. His nose quivered and he jumped up, and then sat down again. The sun gleamed on his white chest and shone on the smooth black fur of his head and back. His soft ears cocked forward expectantly. He lifted one paw.

"All I have is half a sandwich," Sammy said. "I had to eat some because they were watching me. Dogs don't eat fruit, do they? I ate the apple and then Erin ate her Twinkie, but I saved the big half of the sandwich for you."

Jack whined. Sammy unwrapped the sandwich and tossed it down to him. He caught it mid air. Two gulps and it was down his throat. He strained on his leash and looked up at her expectantly. His white tipped tail waved slowly. Once again he whined.

"I don't have any more," Sammy said. "I'm sorry...I'll get you more soon..."

She couldn't do anything else now. Sammy jumped backward off the fence, landing hard.

"Is he okay?" Erin asked.

"I think so. He had fresh water today."

They got their bikes and headed toward the library. Erin had volunteered to help her find the poetry demanded by Mrs. Betancourt. Considering that Sammy wasn't sure where to look, she was grateful for the offer.

Inside, the library was cool and half-hushed. Together the girls wandered up and down the rows of non-fiction shelves. They found auto-repair books, religious books, plays for children, but no poetry.

"People make it up," Sammy insisted. "Maybe it's with the stories."

Erin shook her head. "No. I would have seen it. Let's try on-line."

They found an empty computer terminal. First Erin typed in poetry. There were hundreds of entries. Sammy looked at the clock. It was already quarter to four.

"What were the names again?" Erin squinted at the screen.

"Frost, Browning, and Dylan Thomas," she recited.

Erin tried Frost. There were still dozens of entries.

"What's his first name?"

"How should I know?" Sammy snapped.

Erin turned around to look at her. "You're the one who needs this, not me."

"Sorry."

"Apology accepted." Erin jumped up. "We'd better ask the librarian." She headed across the room toward the information desk. Sammy trailed behind.

"May I help you?" the librarian asked.

Erin smiled and leaned confidently on the desk. "I hope so," she said, "my friend needs some poetry."

"For a school assignment?"

Sammy shook her head. "Not exactly. But I have to find some poems by Frost, Browning and Dylan Thomas. Any poems by them are okay. Do you know who they are?" she asked hopefully.

The librarian's lips quirked. "I think I can ferret them out."

She led them to the 800 section and to two bookcases full of poetry. After a moment of scanning titles, she slid out, *The Classic Hundred*.

"It has poems by each of those poets, and a lot more besides," she explained. "Is this okay, or do you need something more specific?"

Sammy grinned at her. "This is perfect. You saved my life."

"That's my job." The librarian went back to the information desk.

"I'm going to look for some stuff to read," Erin told her. "Call me tonight. I want to hear everything."

Sammy checked out, while Erin hunkered down by the fiction shelves. With the book tucked in her backpack, Sammy hurried out of the library. Mrs. Betancourt would be waiting.

As she followed the afternoon receptionist to Mrs. Betancourt's room, Sammy tried not to wrinkle her nose at the smell. Not exactly a bad smell. More like the wrong smells mixed together – like rose-scented perfume, antiseptic cleaner and stewing onions. It reminded her of the hospital when Papa Jack was sick. Determined, she pushed away the flash of memory. Not now. She had work to do.

This afternoon, Mrs. Betancourt was sitting in a wheelchair by the window. She had a blanket over her knees but her hair was tidily pulled back. The droopy side of her face made her look even stranger than Sammy remembered.

"Mrs. Betancourt," the receptionist chirped, "I've brought Sammy to see you. Isn't that nice!"

Both Sammy and Mrs. Betancourt frowned at the woman's, *"You're old so you must be a deaf idiot"* voice.

"Did you find the poems?" Mrs. Betancourt spoke to Sammy, ignoring the receptionist. Sammy nodded and took the book out of her backpack.

"Let me see."

Sammy held the volume out.

Mrs. Betancourt squinted at it. Her lopsided frown became fiercer. "Read, please."

Sammy wasn't sure what to do. She was sweating now in her jacket, and the only other chair was piled with linen from the bed. So she stood there, in front of the old lady, book open, peeling through the pages in search of a poem by one of the authors Mrs. Betancourt had asked for. Finally she found one.

"Stopping by Woods on a Snowy Evening," Sammy read, "by Robert Frost."

Mrs. Betancourt nodded slightly and closed her eyes. Sammy began to read.

Whose woods these are I think I know.
His house is in the village, though;
He will not see me stopping here
To watch the woods fill up with snow.

My little horse must think it queer
To stop without a farmhouse near
Between the woods and frozen lake
The darkest evening of the year.

He gives his harness bells a shake
To ask if there is some mistake.
The only other sound's the sweep
Of easy wind and downy flake.

The woods are lovely, dark and deep,
But I have promises to keep,
And miles to go before I sleep,
And miles to go before I sleep.

Sammy's voice stopped and for a second or two there was silence. Gradually the sounds of the nursing home permeated her mind. She stopped staring at the poem and looked at Mrs. Betancourt.

The woman's head had rolled sideways and

she was staring out the window. Her careful hair had come undone again. Her eyes looked watery.

"Did I read the poem okay?" Sammy asked in a small voice.

"Again, please."

Sammy read it once more. It was nice – jingly like the horse bells.

"You read it like a young person," Mrs. Betancourt said.

"I am young," she said.

Mrs. Betancourt's head rolled back to look at her. "Do you have any idea what it means?"

Sammy ran her finger up and down the page. "Do you want me to read another poem?"

"No, that one again, please."

Once more Sammy read through the poem. She found herself looking forward to the last few lines. She liked the way the words "sweep of easy wind and downy flake" felt when she said them.

Then the last line was finished. Sammy shifted from one foot to another. All of a sudden this didn't seem like an easy five dollars any more. She wanted to get outside into the cool, clean air. She wanted to get away from this weird old woman.

"I kept my promises," Mrs. Betancourt said wearily. "And I still have miles to go."

"What promises?" Sammy forced her attention back to the old woman.

"You wouldn't understand. You're too young."

Sammy thought about Jack on the end of his chain. "I understand about promises."

Mrs. Betancourt barely nodded her head. "Read me another poem. Read."

Susan Brown

Chapter 10

Treat Him Good

When Sammy got home, the house was deserted. Her mother had left a note on the table and a casserole in the oven.

Erin's mother said you went to the library. You should have called – I do worry, you know. There's home-made lasagna in the oven. Garlic bread is in the fridge. You can heat it up if you want it. I'll be back from my class around 9:15. We'll talk then.

"Great," Sammy muttered. At least she hadn't had to face her mom right off.

When Sammy looked in the fridge, the shelves were practically overflowing. "All right!" she said. "Jack, we're going to do just fine!"

Sammy put all the garlic bread into the oven. Everything smelled great, but the house seemed really empty. For a moment she had a wave of loneliness, for Papa Jack, for her mother, even for the puppy. Resolutely she went into the living room and switched the TV on loud.

When the bread was hot, she took a can of pop, a plate of lasagna and all the bread into her bedroom. Sitting cross-legged on the bed, with the pink bunny beside her, Sammy swirled the hot cheese and tomato sauce around on her tongue. *Mmm.* Papa Jack didn't cook Italian. He said it upset his stomach, all that tomato and cheese. Who knew her mom could make such good lasagna?

Sammy looked approvingly at the pictures on the walls. They were how she had fixed this problem. And her mom had helped, too.

A blob of sauce slipped off her fork and plopped on the sheet. Sammy scooped it up with her finger, and then rubbed the tomato mark. Why hadn't her mom ever helped her before? Was it because Sammy had always gone to Papa Jack? After all, he could fix anything....

She had a sudden memory of him on a hot summer night a year ago. He had picked her up from the pool even though he was really tired from cutting the grass. Her mom had gone away for the weekend with some friends because of the big fight she'd had with her father.

Papa Jack stopped the car but instead of getting out, he just sat there and looked up at their house. The hot night folded in around them, and except for a dog barking far away, everything was really quiet. Sammy sniffed the sharp chlorine smell from her wet bathing suit, the sweet tang of Papa Jack's after-shave, and the overlaid warmth of the new mown grass. She looked over at his face, shadowed like wood in the moonlight.

"You know, Sammy, I've always believed that if you try your best to do right, everything will work out," he'd said.

Sammy wasn't sure what he meant, because he seemed so sad while he said it. She leaned over and put her head on his shoulder. He squeezed her hand. "I know I made mistakes, but I always tried to do what was right. I guess I just have to have faith."

"It'll be fine," she'd said. "I'm getting cold, Papa." So they went in.

Sammy reached for the photo of Papa Jack. Nothing was okay. Nothing was okay at all. But in the photo he was smiling his twinkly smile just like he understood everything. Like everything really would be all right.

She put the photo back, wound her arms around her pink bunny and squeezed hard. She was so busy hugging the stuffed animal and trying not to sink into the kind of "pity party" Papa Jack disliked, that the doorbell rang twice before she was aware of it.

"Who's that?" she muttered.

It was too early for her mother to be back. Erin's parents never let her come over on her own after dark. With a shock of fear, Sammy wondered if she'd locked any of the doors.

The doorbell rang again.

Without turning on any more lights, Sammy glided into the living room. Trying not to make any noise, she pulled back the curtains a crack and squinted out into the night.

Barking, wild, frenzied barking, erupted.

"Jack!" Sammy yelled. She flung open the front door. Brian stood on the porch leaning back against the pull of the leather leash. The moonlight shone on Jack's white bib as he surged toward Sammy.

"Down!" Brian snarled. He used the end of the leash to whip Jack's head.

"Stop!" Sammy cried. Jack didn't seem to notice. Again and again he leaped forward, each time dragged back by the leash. Barking and choking, he hauled Brian into the house.

"Down!" Brian roared. This time he back-handed Jack across the head. The dog stopped, whimpered and lay down at his feet.

"I brought him to you," Brian said abruptly.

"How much money do you have?"

Sammy's eyes darted back and forth between the dog and the boy. "I don't have any yet. Today was my first day, and I don't get paid until the end of the week."

Brian scowled. "The price is still a hundred. If you try and cheat me, I'll get you. You know that, don't you!"

"I'm not going to cheat you!" Sammy's chin shot up.

"You'd better not." Brian dropped down beside the dog and rubbed his head. Jack panted and looked up at him. His tongue darted out and swept across Brian's chin. "You be a good dog or you'll be sorry."

"Why are you bringing him now?"

Brian jammed his hands in his pockets. "I don't want him any more. That's all. I mean, you got to feed him and walk him. Besides, when I go, I'll be moving fast. I won't have time for a dumb mutt. Here. He's yours now." He thrust the end of the leash toward Sammy. "Treat him good."

"I'll treat him fine, Brian."

"Yeah, well. You'd better." Brian turned on his heel and left. The door slammed behind him.

Jack leapt up and flung himself at the door, whining and scratching.

"No, Jack!" Sammy pulled at the leash. Nothing. Jack's big paws scrabbled at the wood, leaving long gouges in the paint.

"No! Mom will kill me!" Sammy dropped the leash, wrapped her arms around Jack's body and tried to pull him back. The dog writhed powerfully in her grip, jerking sideways. Free, he lowered his head, straightened his tail and snarled.

Sammy froze. The growl rose and fell in Jack's throat. Dogs could smell fear. She shouldn't be afraid. But how can you turn off being scared?

She straightened slowly. "Easy boy." Her voice cracked. She swallowed. "Take it easy, Jack. I'm your friend...remember me? I'm Sammy...your friend. I brought you treats. You want a treat now?"

Sammy took a step back. The growl increased in volume. Sammy took a slow breath, then another small step. Jack took a step toward her. Sammy stopped moving.

"We can't stay like this all night." Sammy forced herself to speak in a normal tone. Should she try and sound in charge? How? Frantically Sammy thought about all the in-charge people she knew. Desperately, she decided to act like a teacher – how'd Mrs. Bennett do that?

Sammy slowly put her hands on her hips. She took a deep breath. She lowered her head and looked straight as though she were looking over the top of a pair of glasses. She squeezed her lips into a thin line.

Jack's head tilted a little.

"Just what do you think you're doing?" she said.

Jack's head came up and his ears moved forward, and then back. Pleased, Sammy gave him another teacher look.

"I expect you to behave yourself," she scolded.

Jack's head lowered again. His tail wasn't quite so stiff and straight.

"Now, if you're going to be a good dog..." a small movement of his eyebrows... "I'll get you a treat. For a good dog."

Fighting to control her breathing, Sammy slowly walked toward the kitchen. She jumped when Jack barked sharply, but she kept walking. The trickle of sweat in her back became a river. She heard the soft clicks of Jack's claws on the floor behind her.

She went to the fridge. As she put her hand on the latch, the dog whined. Sammy glanced over her shoulder. Jack sat back on his haunches and slowly lifted one too big paw in the air.

Sammy laughed, high pitched from relief. "Oh Jack, you are so smart!"

The puppy barked. Sammy pulled open the fridge door. Hot dogs. Fingers fumbling, she tore open the package.

Jack was up on his haunches now, both front paws waving. Sammy laughed again. She broke off a piece of the hot dog and tossed it to the puppy. He caught it neatly and gulped it down.

"Good boy!" Sammy crowed. "I knew you were a good dog, Jack!"

Joyfully, she tossed him chunk after chunk of the wiener. When it was gone, she started to put the rest away. Jack barked sharply. Sammy jumped.

"Okay, one more." This time she put the package away first. The dog moved in closer. "Sit!" Sammy commanded. For a moment, she thought Jack would jump at her, but finally he sat and waved his paw again. As she gave him the last piece, she risked rubbing his ears with her other hand. He didn't seem to notice, as he sniffed her palm for one last lick of meat.

"It's going to be fine," Sammy whispered.

Suddenly, Jack's head jerked up. An instant later, Sammy heard the key in the door.

"No!" Sammy cried.

Jack whirled around and lunged toward the hall.

The door opened. "I'm home!" Sammy's mother called.

Sammy and the Devil Dog

112   Susan Brown

Chapter 11

Lonely

"Jack!" Sammy shrieked.

The dog tore away. Sammy hurtled after him – too late. Her mother screamed as Jack sprang toward her. His open mouth raked her sleeve. She staggered and braced herself against the back door. He leaped again.

"Sammy!" Her mother cried. One arm crooked across her face. "Sammy! Are you all right?"

"Mom! Don't move!" Sammy yelled back. "No Jack! *No!* Down!"

The dog didn't even seem to hear. Over and over, he leapt up, slamming the woman with his front legs and chest. As soon as his paws hit the floor he twisted and surged up again, barking, wound up like a spring.

"*Down!*" Linda Connor jabbed the dog's chest hard with her forearm. Jack dropped down for a moment, panting. Sammy tried to grab the leash and then step on it. It whipped around with every movement of the dog. Finally she threw herself forward, trying to encircle his middle. Like a jungle cat, he jumped upwards, out of her arms. The long, feathered tail whipped through her hands. The dragging leash twisted like a snake.

In the second's pause, Sammy's mother raced toward the kitchen. Jack hesitated and then galloped after her. Linda Connor grabbed the broom by the kitchen door and faced the dog. Sammy grabbed for his collar. He jerked around, snapping. Sammy jumped back. Her mother side-stepped toward her, holding the broom in front of them both, forcing the dog back into the kitchen.

"Down! I said down!" Linda Connor swung the broom at the dog, as though sweeping him away in a dust storm. Confused, Jack backed up.

"Go on!" She swung the broom again. The dog retreated farther. "Quick! Open the cellar door," she commanded Sammy.

"Mom, don't hurt him!"

"Open the door!"

Sammy yanked the door open. Her mother shoved the broom at Jack. Barking, he backed up one step, then another, toward the door.

"Go on. Down!"

Abruptly, Jack turned and loped down the cellar steps. Linda Connor slammed the door and sagged against the wall.

"Oh, Sammy...are you all right? He didn't bite you, did he?"

Sammy shook her head and crossed her arms around her body to hide her shaking. "No, he barked a lot, but then I gave him a hot dog. He was really nice, then."

Her mother pushed back her hair. "Really nice is hard to imagine. What is he doing here? How are we going to get rid of him? Maybe the police will take him..."

"No!" Sammy protested. "You don't understand. He's mine. I'm going to keep him."

"Keep him?" Her mother sounded dazed. "What are you talking about? That dog is totally wild."

Behind the cellar door, Jack began to whimper. His paws scrabbled on the wood.

"He's not completely wild. He didn't bite!"

Her mother snorted.

Sammy tried again. "He's only a puppy, Mom – about five months. He's a baby. The boys who had him kept hitting him and throwing firecrackers and stuff at him. He's half-starved and he didn't even have water sometimes. I told you about him before."

"He's vicious." Linda Connor leaned the broom against the wall and slowly sat down at the kitchen table.

Sammy sat down opposite her and leaned forward. "He hasn't had a chance to be anything else. I'm going to teach him to be the best dog in the world. I've already started looking after him."

"Have you, Sammy?" Her mother's lips tightened and her fingernail tapped the table. "Maybe by feeding him your lunch?"

Heat shot into Sammy's face. "Are we having that talk now?"

Her mom nodded. "I think we'd better. You really did a number on me to your principal. I'm expecting some surprise visits any time from Child Protective Services – you know, to find out why I'm starving and neglecting you. How could you do this to me?"

Sammy dropped her eyes. "I didn't mean it to happen. Everything got out of hand."

"I noticed." Her mother's fingers tapped faster.

"Well, at least you noticed something." Sammy shot back.

"What's that supposed to mean, young lady?"

Behind the door, Jack made a sound – a soft howl, like a baby wolf. A lonely, scared, baby wolf.

"All you think about is your stupid pottery!" Sammy shouted. "I have to do everything and fix everything and you don't do anything. Papa

Jack is gone. There's nobody but me to do everything and I can't! I can't! You don't even have a job!"

"A job! I'm an artist, Sammy! Artists have to make sacrifices – you know that!"

"But I'm not an artist. That's just an excuse so you don't have to do anything you don't want to. You don't even shop unless my principal gets after you. I hate you!"

Her mother's hand slammed the table, but her voice quivered. "You are such a spoiled brat. You just don't get it. I've had to look after everything – bills, moving – you! And I miss my father. We made each other mad, but he was always proud of my work. You aren't the only one that things have happened to. I...I..." Her mother got up jerkily and walked out of the room.

Sammy just sat, arms folded over her sick stomach. Jack scratched on the door and whined. Sammy didn't move. She didn't know what to do. Finally, she got up and crossed over to the door. Hearing her, Jack cried and scrabble his claws against the wood.

Sammy left the kitchen. The bathroom door was shut and the shower was running. Behind her, Jack's voice rose to a howl. The heavy old door muffled the sound, but its echoes seemed to rise from the floorboards.

In her room, Sammy threw herself on the bed. She reached for the pink bunny and hugged it fiercely. Now what? Her mother would probably never speak to her again. Sammy pushed that from her mind. She had to do something about Jack. There was no food or water in the cellar. She curled into a tight ball with the bunny against her stomach.

After a while, the shower stopped running. Sammy wondered if her mom would come in and yell at her. Her hand stroked the soft fluff of the bunny.

The back door opened and closed. Her mom had gone out to the pottery studio.

Jack howled again. So lonely.

This time Sammy got up and headed to the kitchen. Through the window, she could see her mother's silhouette in the barn. The shadow swayed back and forth with the rhythm of the potter's wheel.

Wham! The weight of Jack's body shook the door in its frame. Sammy jumped and swallowed.

"Take it easy," she said. The dog barked and whined. Sammy twisted her fingers together. "I'll get you something to eat and drink. You'll like that, won't you, Jack?"

Did he recognize her voice? Did he know she would be nice to him?

Slam...howl...scratch...

Sammy scanned the fridge and chose a slice of ham to remind Jack that she'd been nice to him before.

Slam...howl...scratch...

Crusty lasagna edges and garlic bread into the bowl...topped off with a liberal helping of Cheerios. Her hands were shaking.

Slam...howl...scratch...Slam...howl... scratch...

A hot dog broken in pieces over the pile.

"It looks like a doggy sundae," she told the door. Jack barked.

He'd need water too. She filled a soup dish at the faucet. Holding a bowl in each hand, she hesitated by the door. Once again, she looked through the window toward the barn. She had to do it.

Sammy put the food and water on the floor and then turned the handle to the cellar door.

Leash still trailing, Jack shot out, banging the door, nearly knocking her over.

He barked at her. High pitched. Was he scared too?

Sammy crouched and pushed the bowl of food toward him. Jack's head lowered. His nose quivered. One paw, then another inched forward. He bolted to the food. Sammy fell over backwards. The dog eyed her warily as he gulped the meal. Sammy edged herself upright. Jack paused to bark once and then kept on eating.

When the bowl was thoroughly empty and licked, he looked up at her, tail waving back and forth, very slowly. It was there again – the warm brown look in his eyes. He sat back and panted softly. His tail swished across the floor and once again he looked like an overgrown puppy. The crazy dog was gone.

Sammy held out her hand. Jack cringed back and whined.

"Oh, sweetheart! I'll never hurt you." Instinctively, Sammy crouched down and held out her arms. Slowly Jack's head extended. She held her breath. His nose touched the back of her hand, cool, gentle. His eyes held hers, and her fingers extended to brush the soft tip of his ear.

Abruptly, he jerked back, looked around the room, and spotted the broom leaning against the wall. A mock pounce, a growl, and then Jack got up enough courage to lunge at it. The broom toppled. Jack yelped and jumped backwards. Sammy laughed.

The dog barked and cautiously sniffed at the handle. Apparently satisfied that it was dead, he sat on his haunches, smug triumph on his face.

"You got it, didn't you?"

Jack barked and his tail swished the floor. He looked at her expectantly. Maybe Jack had to go outside. Her mother would get even angrier if the dog made a mess. Keeping her eyes on his, Sammy leaned over and took the end of the dragging leash.

"Want to go for a walk?"

Outside, Jack strained ahead, hard to hold. The pup wove back and forth in front of her, sniffing and yanking every time he caught a whiff of some irresistible smell. Several times he stopped and lifted his leg against a tree.

"You go ahead and mark your territory," Sammy told him. "Because now this is your territory. This is your house and your yard and I'm your owner."

Jack didn't even cock his ears at her voice, but Sammy didn't care. She felt like yelling that she, Sammy, was walking her very own dog.

They went farther and farther, pulled along by Jack's raw energy. By the convenience store, it started to rain – first in big splatters and then in driving sheets. Sammy pulled on the leash. "Come on, Jack. Let's go home."

The dog ignored her. Sammy pulled with all her strength. He didn't move.

"How did you get so strong?" Sammy yanked again. Jack spun around, planted his four feet and leaned backward against the pull of the leash. His head came down. No matter how hard she pulled, she couldn't tip him off balance or make him come.

"Jack," Sammy pleaded. "You don't want to stay out here in the rain, do you?"

Jack barked sharply.

"I have a whole bowl of food for you," Sammy tried. "Mmmm. Yummy!"

Jack's barking became a crescendo of noise. Sammy was ready to weep with frustration. Her hair was sticking to her head and her clothes were sopped. She stopped pulling.

When the leash dropped, Jack relaxed. Thinking he would come now, Sammy turned in the direction of the house. The leash snapped tight again.

Sammy plunked down on the curb, back to the dog. Jack didn't care. He sniffed at a garbage can.

"Go on! Get away from there," a gruff voice muttered.

Sammy turned around. A woman of no age Sammy could tell, left a shopping cart overflowing with boxes and plastic bags and began pawing through the garbage. The rain smeared the grey dirt on her face and beaded on the wool cap jammed over her stringy hair. Her clothes were bulky and torn. Sockless feet shuffled loosely in broken men's shoes. Jack dropped his head and backed toward Sammy without a sound.

The bag lady finished with the garbage and eyed Sammy. "I got no where to live and nothing to eat," she mumbled. "Spare some change?"

Sammy shook her head. "I don't have any money. I'm sorry..."

The woman grunted and slowly pushed her cart away through the rain.

Sammy started to shake. Her face streaked with rain and salty tears, too.

Would that happen to her? She couldn't pay for everything. What would happen when all the money Papa Jack left them was gone? Her mom would have to get work then, wouldn't she?

But, what about that bag lady? She hadn't gotten a job. Did she have a daughter somewhere? Sammy wrapped her arms around herself and head down, rocked slowly back and forth. If she held her breath, she couldn't cry.

A cool nose touched her hand. She startled, turned and then reached for Jack. His thick wet fur brushed her face. Her nostrils were full of his earthy animal smell.

"Oh Jack," she whispered.

He wriggled sharply in her arms, but it was only to twist his head so that his soft, hot tongue could lick her cheek.

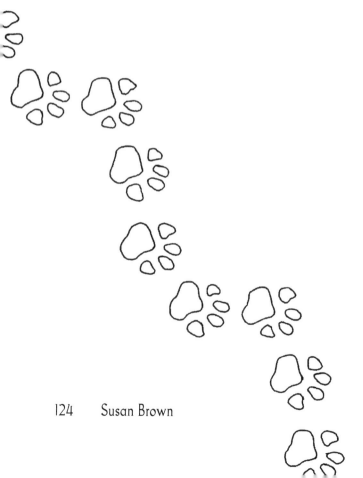

Chapter 12

Your Responsibility

Sammy pressed her face into Jack's fur for a moment longer. Then another intriguing smell caught the dog's attention and he wriggled free. With a parting flip of his tongue across her ear, he loped over to a tree, sniffed it thoroughly and then looked back at her with an inquiring woof.

The rain had not let up. Sammy was soaked.

"C'mon Jack. Let's go home."

Jack trotted along beside her as she jogged back home. When she opened the door, he went right in, allowed her to unsnap the leash and kept on going into the kitchen. He gave a sharp bark at the broom lying on the floor and then sat in front of the refrigerator. He lifted his paw and gazed at Sammy pleadingly.

She laughed. "You are so smart! Do you want more to eat?"

Jack barked. But when Sammy took out a hot dog, he lunged at her hand.

"Ow!" Sammy cried. Jack gobbled the wiener then barked sharply. Biting her lip, Sammy ran cold water over the scratches on her knuckles. That's when her mom came in.

"Sammy, what's he doing out!" She made a wide circle and took Sammy's hand. "He bit you!"

Sammy shook her head. "No, he didn't. He just grabbed a hot dog."

"Why on earth did you let him out of the cellar? Where've you been? You're all wet." Her mom reached into the cupboard for some antiseptic. "Here. Put this on your cut." She surveyed her daughter. "What happened?"

"Nothing." Sammy winced as she poured the solution onto her broken skin. "Jack was crying and I was afraid he had to go to the bathroom. So I took him for a walk to the convenience store and back."

"At night? By yourself?"

Sammy almost laughed. "I had my dog with me."

Her mother frowned. "I guess." She slowly put away the medicine. "Look, Sammy, you know you can't keep him. He's completely wild."

"No he isn't," Sammy protested. "He just hasn't learned to trust us yet. Or behave properly. He licked my face."

"You let him near your face? What if he'd bitten you? You could have been scarred or even lost your sight!" Her mother looked panicked.

"But he didn't. He just needs to be loved and looked after."

Sammy tried to look casual as she rubbed the fur on Jack's shoulder. He lifted his head and panted gently. Then he flopped down on the floor.

Her mother eyed Jack warily and sat down at the table. "No, Sammy. Absolutely not. Dogs cost a lot of money – food, vet bills, licenses." Her mouth settled into a thin line and red spots burned on her cheeks. "As you pointed out, I can barely afford to feed us."

Sammy sat down opposite her mother. Jack's tail thumped a couple of times before he laid his head on his big paws.

"See, Mom. He's not wild. Jack will get better." The dog lifted his head, yawned and then settled again. Sammy took a deep breath. "Besides, I'm going to look after everything."

"Really? How?"

"I have a job."

"You what?"

"I have a job. I read to Mrs. Betancourt," Sammy said. "She's an old lady who's had a stroke and her daughter is paying me five dollars an hour to read to her after school."

She looked pleadingly at her mother. Linda Connor glanced down at the dog, sleeping peacefully on the floor.

"Is it the mother of one of your friends?"

Puzzled, Sammy shook her head. "No. I went to a lot of places and asked if they would hire me. Most of them wouldn't even talk to me. But Papa Jack said the only real losers were quitters, so I kept asking and asking. Then finally Mrs. La Mantea hired me. Wasn't that lucky?"

Her mother tapped the table with her fingertips. "So how often do you read?"

"Every day, after school."

"What about playing with Erin and your other friends? What happens when you're tired of reading to an old lady? Will you just quit?"

Sammy lifted her chin. "I can't quit. Jack is my responsibility."

"So he is." Her mother stood up. "Well, I'm not going to bed with your responsibility loose. Get him downstairs."

Not daring to argue any more, Sammy stood up too. "Come on, Jack. It's bed time."

Heart pounding, teeth clenched, she hooked her fingers under Jack's collar and pulled him to his feet. Sleepily, he allowed her to shoo him downstairs. She grabbed the water dish and set it on the landing before gently closing the door.

"See, Mom, how good he's being!"

Her mother shook her head. "I don't want him, Sammy. He's too wild. We'll talk about it again tomorrow."

"But, Mom..."

"Tomorrow!" Her mother turned and headed toward the bathroom. Sammy switched off the light.

"Good night, Jack. Sleep tight," she whispered.

It seemed to Sammy that she had just fallen asleep when her mother rousted her out of bed.

"Mo..om," she moaned. "It's too early." Blearily she looked at the clock. It was half an hour before her alarm was set.

"Come on." Linda Connor pulled back the blankets. "Your responsibility needs to be taken for a walk before you go to school." She flipped on the lights as she left the room.

Sammy swung her legs out of bed. She kept her head on the pillow though. It seemed too much to move. She groped for her pink bunny, hugged it a moment, and then with huge effort, pulled herself into a sitting position.

Sammy sleepwalked through the morning routine. A shower woke her up finally. She toweled her hair kind of dry, slicked it back, pulled on her shirt and jeans and headed to the kitchen.

Her pleasure at all the choices for breakfast (cereal, muffins, pop tarts...) was spoiled by the sound of Jack alternately hurling himself against the door and howling his misery. Her mother sat at the table, scowling at her coffee.

"Noisy, isn't he?" she remarked.

Sammy took down the leash and opened the cellar door. Mistake. Major mistake.

Jack barreled out, careened around the kitchen, lunged at the broom, then backed into a corner and barked at them. When Sammy reached her hand out to him, he lowered his head and growled.

"Sammy! Be careful!" Her mother started for the broom.

"No, mom! It's okay!" Hands on her hips, Sammy confronted Jack. "Stop that!" she commanded. "For a smart dog you're acting really stupid. Don't you want to go for a walk?"

Jack watched her suspiciously. The growl died. But when she tried to fasten his leash, he snapped at her and backed farther into the corner.

"Sammy..." her mom said.

"It's okay, Mom." Sammy straightened, panic flickering at her mind. If she went too close, Jack might bite her. She could almost feel the hot, painful crunch of his jaws on her arm. If she acted scared, her mom would get rid of him. Think, she commanded herself. Think.

Not knowing what else to do, Sammy went to the fridge. Before she even had the door open, Jack was there, begging. Sammy had a brief flash of understanding of why Brian had clouted his dog. She tightened her lips. She wasn't like Brian and his family. She would use kindness to train Jack.

"Stay!" she commanded. Jack cocked his head and then roughly grabbed the ham from her fingers. But he let her snap on the leash.

"Good boy," she said. Her mother sank back into her chair and grimly picked up her coffee cup.

Tail wagging, Sammy dragging, Jack plunged toward the door.

"Please don't let me be late...please don't let me be late..." Sammy tore down the street toward school. A bell had rung already. If it was the line-up bell she could make it. If it was the last bell, she was dead.

Kids were still being dropped off. But that didn't mean anything. Some kids' parents never got them there on time. She rammed her bike into the rack, locked it, and raced toward her classroom. She burst into the room just as the bell rang.

"Mrs. Bennett," Frank called. "Sammy's late again."

"I am not," Sammy protested.

Mrs. Bennett was saved from answering by the crackle of the PA signaling the morning announcements.

It seemed to Sammy that she was sliding in late on everything that morning. When Mrs. Bennett gave directions about their math groups, Sammy listened and then couldn't remember what she had heard. It was as though her ears worked but her brain had turned off.

When they read aloud, she raised her hand to volunteer and then started at the wrong place.

"Are you okay?" Erin whispered.

Sammy nodded. "I'll tell you later."

Her eyes kept straying to Brian's desk. Empty. Had he left last night for San Francisco?

Sammy felt a thrill of tension. Was she supposed to tell someone about it? Brian said he'd kill her if she told, but didn't the teachers keep saying that that's the time you're supposed to tell?

She was saved from making a decision by Brian showing up just before recess. He looked awful. His eyes were puffy and he kept rubbing his forehead with both hands. He ran his fingers through his hair and then started all over again on his forehead. Was he was sick, Sammy wondered, or maybe feeling really bad about giving up Jack?

Mrs. Bennett came over then and touched the back of her hand to Brian's forehead. "Are you feeling okay?" she asked.

He jerked his head back. "Take your hands off me," he snarled.

He folded his arms on the desk and buried his face. Mrs. Bennett eyed him a moment then went back up to the front of the room. "Okay everybody," she said. "Let's get ready for your spelling test."

Sammy sighed. She'd completely forgotten to study. It looked like she'd be in the room during recess writing out words instead of telling Erin everything that had happened.

They did the test. Brian never lifted his head, let alone his pencil. Mrs. Bennett let him be. Sammy struggled through the list then handed it over to Marc to correct. She got Frank's. She would have liked to mark them wrong, or better still, holler out when he did make a mistake, but it wasn't worth it. He only made one error and it might have just been bad writing.

"Rats!" he said when she handed it back. "My mother will kill me."

"For one mistake?" Marc asked. "Here, Sammy. You'd better study next time."

Eight mistakes. Each one written out five times. Forty words. Recess was definitely gone. The bell rang. Most of the kids put away their books. Meeting Erin's eyes, Sammy shook her head.

"For those of you with more than one mistake," Mrs. Bennett said. "I want them Monday morning in your best cursive – with a sentence showing the meaning for each. I have a meeting today."

She dismissed the tables and the kids flowed outside. Brian roused himself too, and bulldozed through the kids making their way to the playground. He just laughed at the howls of fury when he stepped on kids' feet or shouldered them into the doorjamb.

"Why doesn't Mrs. Bennett do something," Frank complained.

"She's probably hoping I'll squash you like a bug!" Brian batted him heavily on the top of the head.

"Ow! Mrs. Bennett!" But the teacher had already left the room.

"Let's get out of here," Sammy whispered to Erin. She didn't want to be near Brian in case he demanded his money or his dog. She didn't want to get clouted or stepped on either.

Together, she and Erin slipped away from the crowd of kids and circled around behind the building. Technically it was out of bounds, but Mrs. Patel, the playground aide, just smiled and waved when she saw them sitting on the grass, backs against the brick wall.

"Mrs. Patel is so nice," Erin said as she settled in. "So, did you read to that old lady last night?"

"Mrs. Betancourt? Yes," Sammy said. "But guess what? I have Jack!"

"Seriously?"

"Yup. Brian brought him over after I got home." Then Sammy told Erin how Jack had run wild all over the house.

"Oh my gosh," Erin exclaimed. "Weren't you scared?"

"Totally. I was sure he would bite me, but he didn't." Sammy shifted. "But I've still got a huge problem. My mom really wants to get rid of Jack, but I kept saying I would look after everything."

"So?"

"So, I have to buy dog food and a bowl and a license and everything for Jack, but I promised Brian I would give him the money as soon as I got paid."

Erin thought about it. "Pay Brian. He's a bad person to have mad at you."

"Then what am I going to feed Jack? If I ask my mother, she'll say that proves I can't look after him and he's gone."

"Oh." Erin frowned. "Then you'll just have to pay for both."

Sammy rolled her eyes. "I know that. But I can't pay for both. I don't have enough money."

Erin sighed. "Well, I could get some of Casey's dog food for you. We buy it in fifty pound bags, so there's lots."

"It doesn't seem right, because I said I'd do it."

"It's your decision."

Just then the bell rang. Back in the classroom, it was a relief when Mrs. Bennett had them open their social studies textbooks. Sammy was really tired of thinking. They were half way through the discussion questions when Mrs. Martinez appeared at the door.

"I'm sorry to interrupt, Mrs. Bennett," she said. "I need to take Brian out of class."

Everyone's eyes turned toward the door.

"Oh wow!" Frank crowed. "You're going to get it now, Brian."

Behind Mrs. Martinez stood two police officers.

Sammy and the Devil Dog   137

138   Susan Brown

Chapter 13

Secrets

Brian's face paled. He clutched his textbook as though it would protect him. "What?" he demanded.

"Please come down to the office, Brian," Mrs. Martinez said. "Right now."

Sammy looked back and forth between them, feeling sick. Brian sank further into his chair and spread his big arms over the desk as though bracing himself to be pulled away forcibly.

"No," Brian said. "I don't want to."

"Now, Brian," Mrs. Martinez ordered. Hot red spots burned in her cheeks.

Brian looked around the room, eyes big. Most of the kids just looked at him with scared expressions. Frank was grinning. Mrs. Bennett moved smoothly to Brian's side and crouched so that she could speak to him at eye level.

"Better go, Brian," she said. "Help Mrs. Martinez straighten things out."

"It isn't fair," Brian yelled. "Everybody always thinks I did everything. I hate all of you!"

He lurched out of his desk and, fists jammed in his pockets, went with Mrs. Martinez and the officers.

"He does do everything," Frank crowed. "This is so cool!"

"Frank," Mrs. Bennett said. "Shut up."

After that, no one seemed much interested in explorers. Mrs. Bennett finally wrote some fraction problems on the board and told the kids to work on them until lunch recess.

When the bell rang, Sammy would have headed outside with the rest of the kids. Everybody was still full of nervous energy. She could hear the high pitch of her classmates' voices as they shouted about the games.

"Wait, Sammy!" Erin caught her arm. "You're supposed to see Mrs. Sovich again, aren't you?"

Sammy pulled her arm back. "She would have called me if she really wanted me to come."

"Are you sure?" Erin worried. "What if you get in trouble?"

"You mean more trouble." Sammy snapped, but she went to the office.

Mrs. Pope and Mrs. Sovich were deep in conversation. "Something has to be done,"

Mrs. Pope said. "That poor boy. He's not like those brothers of his. He has a good heart."

Mrs. Sovich shrugged. "I don't know about them. But Brian's headed for serious trouble."

"If he isn't there already. It makes me so angry...." They noticed Sammy then.

"Oh, Sammy," Mrs. Sovich said. "I'd forgotten we had an appointment. Go on in."

Sammy started to go and then stopped. "Mrs. Pope, is Brian okay?"

The office manager hesitated. "Yes, he's gone home."

"The police didn't arrest him, did they?"

Mrs. Pope shook her head. "No, they just wanted to ask him about some break-ins near his house. They thought he might have noticed something."

Sammy was sure there had to be more to it than that, but she was also sure Mrs. Pope wouldn't lie to her. Reluctantly, she turned toward the counselor's office. She caught a glimpse of Mrs. Martinez on the phone in her office. There was no sign of the police officers.

Slowly, Sammy took her lunch out of a paper sack and arranged it in front of her. She had a sandwich, carrot sticks, four cookies, grapes, a chocolate chip granola bar, a box of fruit juice and a paper napkin. With her mom's help, she had made it after Jack had been walked and fed more ham, cheese and Cheerios. Sammy had felt a flush of gratitude that her mother didn't say anything about the expensive meat Jack had been gobbling down.

As Sammy looked at the display of food in front of her, she wasn't sorry her mom had gone shopping. But yesterday's meetings with the principal and Mrs. Sovich made her squirm. Somehow it didn't seem right that Sammy'd gotten her mom in trouble.

Mrs. Sovich came in and fussed around her office. "Well, Sammy, how's it going today?"

"Fine." Sammy had the feeling Mrs. Sovich couldn't quite remember why she was there. Then her eyes focused on Sammy's array of food. Her eyebrows lifted. Sammy sat straight up, feeling the heat spread across her face.

"Nice lunch," Mrs. Sovich said.

Sammy nodded. "Mrs. Sovich..." Her voice was wavering. "...I was really mad at my mom yesterday about...about a lot of things. But she isn't mean to me. And I feel really bad about the things I said."

"Were the things you said true?"

Sammy felt panic rising. "No...yes...sort of...but not really." She took a deep breath. "I just shouldn't have said that stuff."

"But you did say it, Sammy," Mrs. Sovich said. "If it's true, we need to help you. If it isn't true, then we need to find out why you're feeling the way you do."

"I know how I feel."

"That's good. Let's talk about it, shall we?"

Sammy gazed at her helplessly. She could almost hear the rattle of the chain.

Mrs. Sovich didn't let her out until the bell for classes rang again. Then Mrs. Bennett kept them working at their desks all afternoon.

The last bell had rung and they were headed to the bike racks before Sammy could tell Erin about the meeting.

"How was it?"

"I think I'll kill myself," Sammy replied. "It will save my mother the trouble. Mrs. Sovich thinks we should all meet together and talk in her office. I don't know what to do now."

"Wow," Erin said. "If I were you I'd start thinking seriously about running away from home."

Sammy giggled. "I'll have to go to San Francisco with Brian."

"What? Why has Brian gone to San Francisco? Because of the police?"

Too late, Sammy remembered that no one but she knew Brian's plans. Desperately she cast around for something to tell Erin.

Everything but the truth seemed like it would get her into more trouble. The truth would do that too. Her and her big mouth.

"I'm not supposed to tell..."

"You know I'll keep the secret." Erin leaned closer, smiling in anticipation. Sammy wasn't so sure. Erin was the kind of person who thought she didn't tell secrets, but somehow they would slip out anyway. Kind of like mine did just then, Sammy thought. She fussed with her bike lock to buy time.

"Brian's mom lives in San Francisco," she said finally. "He wants to go stay with her, that's all."

Erin sat back, disappointed. "That's no big deal. If I had brothers like Brian's, I'd want to live anywhere else. Can I come over and see Jack?" She fastened her helmet and pulled her bike from the rack. "We could work on our science projects."

"I can't," Sammy said regretfully. "I have to read to Mrs. Betancourt. Could you come over later? Around four-thirty or five. I'll be home by then."

Erin shook her head. "No. My Mom won't let me come that late. I'll call you tonight. See you." She hopped on her bike and with a wave, rode off.

Sammy strapped on her own helmet and pushed off. It only took about ten minutes to get to the nursing home.

Inside, the receptionist smiled at her. "Mrs. Betancourt's waiting for you. Go on down to her room."

Once again Sammy wrinkled her nose at the smell in the hallway. At a distance she could hear somebody crying dismally. Isn't anybody happy anywhere, she wondered.

Mrs. Betancourt was sitting in her wheelchair. There was a small bouquet of flowers on the windowsill behind her. Too pretty for this place.

"Hello, Mrs. Betancourt." Sammy shed her backpack and got out the poetry book. Today she perched on the side of the bed facing the old lady.

"So you're back," Mrs. Betancourt said in her slurry voice.

Sammy nodded. "I said I'd come every day, except weekends."

The old woman snorted. "You'll get tired of it."

Sammy wanted to say she was tired of it now. Instead, she asked what she should read.

"Read 'Stopping by Woods on a Snowy Evening' again," Mrs. Betancourt commanded. "You have a nice voice, Samantha," she added.

Surprised, Sammy found the poem and read again. She had memorized almost half of it now, so she stole looks at Mrs. Betancourt. The old woman's eyes had closed and her breathing seemed more even. Sammy was reminded again of Papa Jack as he lay in the hospital. No wonder Mrs. La Mantea had been so weepy.

Was Mrs. Betancourt going to get better? Sammy faltered on the words. The old woman's eyes opened. Sammy stopped reading abruptly.

"What is it?" Mrs. Betancourt asked.

"When...when will you be able to go home?" Sammy asked.

Mrs. Betancourt looked at her for a moment, and then smiled crookedly. "Soon, I hope," she said. "I hope it will be soon. Please read it again."

Reassured, Sammy lifted the book and began again at the beginning.

A little later, Mrs. Betancourt fell asleep. Sammy wasn't sure what to do, so she began flipping through the book of poems and reading aloud the ones that appealed to her. Most of them seemed long, serious, and boring, but she found some that were funny or exciting. She read them out loud, just in case Mrs. Betancourt woke up. Besides, she didn't have anything else to do.

The hour had nearly passed according to the little clock on the nightstand, when Sammy heard someone at the door.

"That was very nice," Mrs. La Mantea said softly. "How's my mother?"

Sammy flushed. "She fell asleep. I didn't know if I should keep reading or not."

Mrs. La Mantea smiled. "Thank you. The nurse told me that already mother was brighter. She was so pleased. And I am so grateful."

Sammy smiled and felt herself blush even more.

"I owe you for two days reading, don't I?"

Sammy nodded.

"I won't be able to get here next Friday before you leave, so I thought, seeing as you're so reliable, that I'll pay you now for next week. Would that be all right?"

Sammy wanted to leap up for joy. "Yes," she said instead, "that would be fine. I mean...if you want to."

"I do." Mrs. La Mantea opened her purse and counted out several fives and tens. "Here you are," she said. "Thirty-five dollars."

"Thank you." They stood there self-consciously. Sammy saw the hour was up so she picked up her backpack. "Well, good-bye. Thank you."

Sammy and the Devil Dog   147

As she left she saw Mrs. La Mantea lean over and kiss Mrs. Betancourt's doughy cheek. "Hi Mom," she said. "I'm here."

Mrs. Betancourt opened her eyes and gripped her daughter's hand. "You're early, Darlene. That's nice...."

Susan Brown

Chapter 14

Mutated Dust Bunnies

Sammy felt like she was soaring on her way home. Thirty-five dollars! She could probably buy dog food and still give twenty-five to Brian. She giggled. Did that mean she had officially bought one of Jack's legs? Or maybe his head and one paw – the one he waved in the air to beg with.

She wanted to get home to him, but the thought of paying the first installment on her pup was irresistible. Brian's house was practically on the way. And besides, she wanted to make sure he was there – that the police hadn't kept him after all.

Instead of climbing the fence at the back, Sammy circled the block to the front of Brian's house. A couple of beat-up cars with their hoods open were parked on the weedy lawn. Joe and Kyle, grease streaked up to their elbows, were leaning under one of the hoods. She could hear their loud jokes and guffaws as they talked and tinkered with the engine.

Sammy suddenly wondered if this was such a good idea. Her chin shot up. Who cared about those guys? Besides, they had no reason to bother her.

She left her bike as far from them as she could, anyway. With only one or two nervous glances in their direction, she walked up to the front door. The doorbell looked broken, so instead she knocked.

Nothing.

She knocked a little harder, then harder again. She could hear the blaring sounds of a computer game. It was punctuated with staccato shouts and explosions. On the fourth knock, Brian's brothers looked over at her. At the same time, Brian came to the door.

"What?" he demanded through the screen. His face still looked puffy to Sammy, like he'd been crying.

"You okay?" she asked.

"What d'you care?"

Sammy shrugged. "I was just asking. What did the cops want?"

Brian scowled at her. "None of your business."

"Excuse me for trying to be nice. Anyway, I got paid. I thought I'd pass on the first installment to you. Twenty-five dollars."

"Oh, yeah?" Brian sounded happy for the first time. He opened the screen door and stepped out onto the porch.

"Here you are!" She offered the bills to Brian. As he reached for them, a sudden shift in his expression caused her to turn around. Joe and Kyle stood behind her.

"Hey, Brian, you never said you had a girlfriend," Kyle mocked.

"I'm not his girlfriend," Sammy retorted. "Why don't you go drop a car on your head or something?" Not a smart thing to say, but she really hated them.

Joe laughed and plucked the bills from her fingers. "So I'll take this for damages."

Sammy tried to snatch it back. "That's not yours!" she shouted. "Give it back."

"Ooh!" Kyle jeered. "Are you gonna make him? Or is your little boyfriend, Brian?"

Brian turned on his heel and slammed into the house. Sammy burned with rage.

"That doesn't belong to you! Or do you slimeballs steal from your own brother?" Sammy demanded. "That money is Brian's!"

Joe leaned against the wall. "We'll give it to him...if you tell us why you're paying him off?"

"I'm not." Sammy felt a jolt of fear. If they found out she had Jack, would they come after him? "It's um...Brian's money. I owed it to him."

"Why?" Joe demanded. His eyes were like stone chips.

Now what? Sammy moved to leave, but Kyle stepped in her way. Another plan, quick. The boys at school were always trading sports cards. "Well, um...Brian sold me some baseball cards."

"For twenty-five bucks?" Kyle sounded incredulous.

"He said that's what they were worth...." Sammy couldn't believe how stupid this sounded. She just hoped Joe and Kyle were dumb enough to buy it.

"Where do you get this kind of cash for baseball cards?" Joe was smiling now, looking almost friendly. That scared Sammy even more.

"My allowance," she blurted.

"Where do you live?" Kyle demanded. "That you get an allowance like that?"

"In the subdivision by the golf course," Sammy said. "All the kids who live there get a huge allowance...I mean it costs a lot...for music and movies...and games...and stuff. All the parents are super loaded and so that's what every kid gets. Twenty-five or thirty a week. Some get more..."

"And what about you?" Joe's eyes had narrowed down into slits. He kept smiling though. Not attractive.

"I live there, don't I?"

Sammy knew she was babbling, but she really wanted to get away. It was turning dark. What if these boys decided to hit her? Would anybody see?

"I gotta go," Sammy declared. With a quick movement she stepped backwards, spun around and darted through the mostly dead flower garden. When she was out of reach, she called back. "You'll give that to Brian, won't you?"

"Oh yeah, for sure!" Joe slid the bills into his pocket. Then whistling, he and Kyle went back to their car.

Sammy picked up her bike, and bounced it over the curb. Brian would never see that money.

It was fully dark when she got home. Lights were on in the barn, but not in the house. If Mom had left Jack in the cellar all day, he must be frantic by now.

Sammy felt a wave of guilt. She should have put him in the yard. But the leash was so short and she hated the idea of tying him up again. When she went into the house, Jack barked and hurled himself against the cellar door.

"I'm coming, Jack," she called. "Just a minute." She really had to use the bathroom.

As she dashed down the hallway, balls of white fluff stuck to her shoes and pant legs. They were all over the place. Even in the bathroom, puffballs were scattered around the toilet and the base of the sink. Mutated dust bunnies? Sammy giggled.

Sammy pushed at the fluff with her toe. Where did this come from? Somehow she didn't think her mom had been having a pillow fight. Curiously she went down the hall. The bedroom doors were shut. Weird. She knocked and then looked in her mom's room. Muddy paw prints patterned the sheets on the unmade bed.

"Uh oh," Sammy said aloud. Well, at least she knew her mom hadn't left Jack in the cellar all day. For that kind of mud, he'd been outside, probably to the creek a couple of blocks away.

Sammy stripped the sheets off her mom's bed and stuffed them in the clothes hamper. Making beds was a pain, but facing her mom about this mess would be worse. Wishing she had someone on the other side to help, Sammy struggled the fitted corners of the clean sheets over the mattress edges.

"You owe me, Jack," she muttered when the bed was finally remade. She surveyed the rest of the room. It looked okay. Her mom was pretty tidy about her stuff, so there didn't seem to be anything else messed up or out of place. Sammy got a cloth and wiped at one spot on the mat that looked like mud. It came cleaner, but smelled of chocolate.

Sammy smiled. Naughty! Her mom must've been eating chocolate fudge ice cream in bed.

She left her mom's room, shutting the door behind her. The fluff was still unaccounted for. Sammy opened her own door.

Muddy paw prints on the bed. The stack of clean clothes toppled and walked on. Stuffed animals every which way. More clouds of white stuffing.

"Jack, how could you do this?" Sammy demanded. In the cellar, Jack barked loudly.

She stripped the bed and remade it. Then she looked carefully at her clothes. A few of them were just rumpled, not dirty, so she put those away. The muddy ones went into the hamper with her sheets. Then she arranged the stuffed animals on her newly made bed.

Sammy stepped back to study the effect. Something was wrong...something was missing...

Her pink bunny! Where was her bunny!

"Mom!" Sammy yelled, "Mom!"

Sammy tore through the house, looking for a mound of pink plush. Nothing. She banged out of the kitchen and raced to the studio. Her mom was putting some bowls in the kiln.

"Mom, did you see my pink bunny?"

Her mom pushed back her hair, leaving a grey streak of powder. "I made the mistake of trying to take your dog for a walk. He got it – after he tore up the rest of the house."

"How? Why did you give him my bunny? Papa Jack gave him to me at Easter. It's special! How could you!"

"I didn't give that dog anything. He ran wild – you saw what he did. And then he topped it off by grabbing your stuffed animal. He snarled at me when I tried to get it back. I thought he was going to bite me." She shut the door of the kiln. "Sammy, this isn't working…"

Sammy sank down on the floor, wrapped her arms around her knees and lowered her head on them. She squeezed her eyes, clenched her teeth. It was only a stuffed animal. The dog didn't know. It was just a piece of fuzzy material with white fluff inside…it was the last present Papa Jack had given her.

"…that dog is completely uncontrollable, and I think we'd better…" her mother's voice stopped. "Are you okay?"

Sammy was aware of her mom crouching down opposite and her fingers stroking her hair. She smelt the earthy tang of clay on her mother's hands as they brushed her face. Sammy looked up and forced a smile.

"I had a really bad day," she said. "And I really liked that bunny."

Her mom nodded. Sammy felt a surge of gratitude followed by a rush of fear. What if her mom was right about Jack? He was wild and maybe Brian's brothers had ruined him – like they were ruined....

"What happened that made it such a bad day?"

Sammy uncurled herself and leaned against her mom's shoulder. "I had to see the counselor again. I tried to tell her I was just mad about the food, but she wouldn't listen and now she wants to see us both to talk about it..."

Her mother stiffened. "Not a chance!"

Sammy nodded. "I tried to tell her but she never listens. Then I read to Mrs. Betancourt which was fine because her daughter paid me for the whole next week. The nurses told her how responsible I was."

Her mother smiled but didn't look happy. "They were right."

Sammy hesitated, not sure what her mother was thinking. She plunged on. "But then I went to Brian's house to pay him part of the money for Jack, like I promised, and..." She suddenly found it hard to keep going.

"And what?" her mom asked.

"And his older brothers took the money. I don't think they'll give it to him. I didn't know what to do, so I came home. I changed the beds."

"Oh, baby, you did have a rough day." Her mom squeezed her arm. "Would it help if we got pizza?"

"Can we afford it?" Sammy felt her stomach constrict at the thought of spending money. What if there wasn't any more? How would they eat?

Her mother shrugged and stood up. "Who cares? I'm sick of scrimping all the time like we're so poor."

"You told me we are. You told me all the money went on bills."

Her mom looked away. "Well most of it did. There's still some. Enough for a pizza, for Pete's sake."

"Mom, what happens when it's gone?" Sammy held her breath.

Linda Connor fussed with the kiln some more. "One of the artists at the college – Randy Sands – likes my work. Maybe he'll help me arrange a show. He's been hinting about something coming up."

"What?"

"Honestly Sammy, if I knew I'd tell you." Her mom sat down on the stool by the potter's wheel, threw a blob of clay in the center and started the wheel spinning. Her strong hands folded over the clay and a smooth form began to rise. "I'm not like you. And I'm certainly not like my father was. I just can't be worrying all the time. I wish you'd understand that."

"I understand, Mom." Sammy rose to her feet and headed toward the door. "It's okay. I have a job. I'll look after things."

"Now, Sammy," her mother said, "that's not what I meant..."

But Sammy had already gone to take care of Jack, so she didn't see Linda Connor smack the clay flat on the wheel and sit staring at the shapeless lump.

160   Susan Brown

Chapter 15

They Were Here

"Okay, I'll meet you at the corner of Maple and 43rd," Erin agreed.

Sammy hung up the phone and turned to Jack, who was nosing around the corners of the kitchen for dropped crumbs and scraps.

"Guess what, boy?" Jack's head lifted momentarily, his tail wagged a couple of times and his ears pricked forward. Then he saw a likely speck and went back to the corner. Sammy ignored his rudeness and got down the leash.

"We're going to go for a walk with Erin and her dog," she said.

At the word "walk" Jack's head shot up. His brown eyes held a look of desperate hope. Sammy laughed and shook the leash. "Want to go for a walk?"

Jack leaped up and thumped her chest with his paws. He barked ecstatically; he ran in circles around the kitchen.

"Okay, sit," Sammy commanded.

Jack leaped on her again.

"Oof!" Sammy gasped at the impact. "I said 'sit'." Jack jumped backwards and barked. "If you don't sit, I can't put on the leash and I can't take you for your walk. Get it?"

Jack didn't get it. He tore from the kitchen and raced around the house, barking wildly. He caught up the remains of the pink bunny from behind the sofa and kept on running. Sammy sat on the sofa in the living room and waited. A moment later, Jack raced back, flopped down in front of her and whined.

"If you're ready to sit still, I'll put your leash on, and we can go," Sammy said. Jack remained lying on the floor, so Sammy knelt by him, ready to snap the fastener onto his collar. The second her fingers hooked around the leather at his neck, his jaws closed over her hand. Sammy resisted the urge to yank her arm back. She'd found out the hard way, that his teeth would leave gouges in her flesh.

"Jack," she said forcing her voice to be calm, "you know I won't hurt you. That's a good boy. Good dog. Jack's a good puppy...." Her voice dropped to a crooning chant. With her other hand, she attempted to attach the leash.

Jack's eyes twitched nervously at the jingling sound at his neck. But he lay still, his teeth firmly gripping her hand.

"Are you holding me hostage," Sammy whispered. "You want to make sure I don't hurt you, don't you, sweet boy? I won't ever hurt you. Jack's a good dog and Sammy loves him...even if you do kill pink bunnies."

Finally she got the lead attached. "All done," she said. "Want to go for a walk?"

Jack leapt to his feet, dropping her hand. Sammy smiled in relief and wiped it on the leg of her jeans. Pleased, she saw there were only a couple of welts. No broken skin.

"We're getting better at this," Sammy told him. Jack pulled toward the door.

With Jack in the lead, they raced down the driveway toward the road. It was only three blocks to their meeting place with Erin and her dog, Casey. Sammy and Jack ran all the way. They got there in time to see her friend and her pet turning the far corner.

Jack's ears pricked forward at the sight of the other dog. His whole body trembled and he strained against the leash.

"It's okay," Sammy said. "We'll just wait here for them." But Jack wasn't having any of it. He barked sharply and plunged ahead. The leash yanked out of Sammy's hand. Jack raced down the road toward Erin and Casey.

"Jack, no! Wait!" Sammy shouted.

Jack came at the golden retriever like a speeding train. Casey watched in bewilderment. At the last moment, Jack swerved and circled behind. He erupted into cascades of barking.

Casey barked once, sharply. Jack crouched low and barked louder. Casey barked again and turned around to face him.

"Sit, Casey," Erin commanded. Her dog started to sit, then thought better of it as Jack began to circle, barking menacingly. Casey lowered her head and growled.

Sammy reached them and grabbed Jack's leash. With her hands on her hips, Erin faced him.

"Behave yourself, Jack!" she scolded. "Casey's your friend."

Both dogs flattened their ears and growled.

Sammy hauled Jack back. "This may not work," she shouted over the din.

"Of course it will," Erin declared. "They just have to get to know each other. Pull Jack back so that they can just touch noses."

Using every ounce of strength, Sammy hauled back her dog. "Quiet," she panted.

"Now Jack, you sit," Erin commanded. Jack hopped around as if he knew what he was supposed to do, but really did not want to do it. "Okay, Casey," Erin said, "you go introduce yourself to Jack."

She allowed her dog a little slack on the leash. The golden retriever stepped forward and leaned out so that her nose was a fraction of an inch from Jack's. Jack jerked back his head and then cautiously leaned forward until their snouts just barely touched. Then, quivering with excitement, their noses ran over each others cheeks, foreheads, necks, and chins several times. Casey strained forward a little more and moved to the rest of Jack's body. Jack stood nervously, allowing the older dog to come close and sniff at the base of his tail. And then he too sniffed some.

Suddenly both plumy tails were waving vigorously, and their tongues were lolling happily. The dogs looked at the girls as though saying, "What are you two waiting for?"

"Told you!" Erin said smugly. "Let's go to the green belt."

They walked another four blocks to the dense stretch of trees that wove through the city. Once on the gravel path, the dogs trotted happily ahead of them.

"Oh guess, what," Erin said. "I know why the cops came for Brian."

"Why?" Sammy demanded. "How'd you find out?"

"Well," Erin said, "my Mom's best friend is the manager at Webster's over at the mall."

"Yeah," Sammy said. Papa Jack had often taken her to the department store. "So?"

"So, they were broken into on Thursday night. The thieves threw something through the window and then grabbed a bunch of watches and coats and stuff. The alarms didn't go off."

"So why'd the police want to talk to Brian?"

Erin raised her eyebrows. "Because the store has video cameras. The burglars wore ski masks and they smashed the camera right away so the tapes weren't very good. But there were three guys, and they thought one of the thieves might be Joe, Brian's oldest brother. Did you know he's already got a record?"

Sammy shook her head. "No."

"He does," Erin said with relish. "And my mom has this other friend whose son got arrested with Joe a year ago for breaking into a house. My mom's friend says Joe made her son do it. That he was a good kid before he became friends with Joe. Joe's on drugs, she says."

"Drugs?" Sammy felt faintly sick. "Does anybody know?"

Erin shrugged. "I don't know. Joe dropped out of school. I don't think the other brother ever goes either."

"Kyle is a snake." Sammy shivered at the memory of Kyle waving his fist at Brian's face. "Do the cops think Brian knows something about the robbery?"

Erin looked at Sammy in surprise. "Sammy, don't you get it? The cops think Brian was part of the robbery. Three thieves. Three brothers. They just don't have proof. Yet."

Sammy stopped. Jack turned to look at her inquiringly. When he strained against the collar, she began moving forward again.

"But that's not right!" Sammy insisted. "Brian's not bad. It's all his brothers. Doesn't anybody care?"

"I doubt it," Erin replied. "Brian's been a pain for a thousand years. I mean, look at how he's always bugging everyone, and beating on them and giving Mrs. Bennett grief when she's trying to be nice to him."

Sammy looked ahead at Jack. The dog was staring intently at a dragonfly. Erin noticed too, and giggled. "Jack is so cute. He'll be the best dog once he calms down and knows he's safe. Next to Casey, of course." Erin paused to rub her dog's ears. Casey panted up at her happily.

The insect flitted away and Jack bounded ahead, jerking Sammy after him. A moment later they came to the road that edged the green belt.

"Now what?" Sammy asked.

"Let's go over to the mall," Erin suggested.

"We can't go in with the dogs."

"I know, but I've spent my allowance anyway," Erin said. "We can look in the outside windows. Maybe we'll see where the break-in was."

It was nearly a mile to the mall. Even Jack was less energetic by the time they got there. Sammy was grateful that he confined his activities to thrusting his nose at everyone who went by. He only barked once at an old lady.

"Sorry," Sammy said. "He's just a puppy."

"You shouldn't be out with a vicious dog like that," the lady snapped.

"She probably has cats," Erin giggled. "Lots of them."

They spent a while looking at the clothes in the window of the Old Navy store. "I'm going to get my Mom to buy me those jeans," Erin said.

"They'll look great on you," Sammy agreed. They'd look great on me, too, she thought. But she wouldn't be getting anything new for a long, long time. And what was she supposed to do if she grew another inch?

"Let's go look in Webster's windows," she said to Erin.

They wandered toward the back of the mall where Webster's had a big display window. It was pretty obvious that was where the break-in had been.

One big section of glass beside the doors was gone and a sheet of raw plywood had been set over it. The shattered glass had mostly been swept up, but splinters glinted in the cracks of the sidewalk. Streaks of greasy black powder, maybe from fingerprinting, clung to the door frame.

Jack nosed at the edges of the window and door. His ears pricked up, then flattened. He pulled his head down between his shoulders and a low growl issued from his lips. His tail shot straight out behind him.

Sammy's stomach tightened.

"What's he growling at?" Erin asked. "It's just wood."

"He smells them," Sammy said tightly. "He smells Brian's brothers. They were here!"

Chapter 16

Devil Dog

"Are you sure!" Erin demanded. She looked at Jack still sniffing and growling. "Is that proof that Brian's brothers broke into the store? You can tell the police and have them arrested!"

"No!" Sammy snapped. "Let's get out of here. Come on, Jack!" Without waiting for Erin, Sammy sprinted away from the store. Jack loped beside her. What if Brian got nailed too? She couldn't stand the idea of him being that bad. The office manager, Mrs. Pope, said Brian had a good heart. How could someone with a good heart become bad?

"Sammy, wait!" Erin and Casey ran to catch up. Sammy didn't slow down but then Jack smelled something new and jerked her around backwards.

"You have to tell the police," Erin insisted when she caught up. "I mean, it could be evidence."

"My dog growling at a broken window is not evidence!" Sammy said. "Besides, what if they think Brian was part of it?"

They stopped by a curb. Erin tugged on Casey's leash. The dog stopped immediately. Jack barked menacingly at a car full of kids.

"If Brian did it," Erin said, "he should be arrested. It's only fair."

"It isn't fair," Sammy argued. "It isn't his fault he got born into that family. They might have made him do it."

Erin shrugged. "Nobody made Brian hit that third grader in the face last year. He isn't nice, Sammy."

"He gave me Jack, when he wanted to keep him."

But Erin had spotted some of their friends from school and was waving them over. Everybody admired Jack until he jumped up and tore Greta's sleeve with his sharp teeth.

"No," Sammy scolded. "Bad dog! Be nice!"

Jack panted up at her happily. He didn't seem to care that he wasn't nice.

It was well after lunchtime when Sammy got back to the house. Her mom had left a note on the table saying she was having coffee with her friend Randy from the college. Erin left right away because she had a two o'clock piano lesson.

"You really embarrassed me, you know," Sammy told Jack as she made herself a peanut butter sandwich. "What was I supposed to tell Greta? I haven't got the money to buy her a new shirt. I spent it all on dog food." Sammy nudged Jack's new food dish brimming with crunchy nuggets. "Which you aren't even eating."

Jack, ignoring the bowl in the hope that something better would appear, alternated between sharp, encouraging barks and paw-waving beggary.

"No way," Sammy told him. "This sandwich is mine."

She sat down at the kitchen table and sorted through the newspapers piled there. That was something they could save money on, Sammy thought – but weirdly her mom wouldn't give them up. Papa Jack was the one who read the newspapers instead of looking online for news.

Sammy sighed and then was distracted by Jack again. Finding that his begging wasn't working, Jack went under cover. From beneath the table, he slid his warm head onto her lap and raised his brown eyes to hers.

"You have no pride," Sammy told him.

A gentle whimper was the response.

Sammy laughed. "Oh all right!" She tore off half her sandwich and offered it to Jack. He snatched it from her fingers, leaving a couple of welts.

"Ow! You need to work on your technique." Sammy picked up the other half and chewed while she thumbed through the day before's paper. There it was, a boxed story about the break-in at Webster's:

Burglars hit Webster's

Burglars threw a car jack through a window of the Webster's store at Highland Shopping Center overnight Thursday and made off with an estimated $2300 worth of merchandise.

The break-in occurred sometime between 9:30 p.m. Thursday and 7:10 a.m. Friday, a police spokesman said.

Items taken include high fashion sportswear and gold jewelry.

In addition to the Webster's burglary, police are looking at possible connections to several nighttime robberies of local stores and a rash of home break-ins.

Sammy swallowed the last bite of her sandwich. Jack gave up and curled on the floor beside her, tail covering his nose.

She read the article again. If Brian had been part of those other nighttime break-ins, he would have been falling asleep in school. Joe and Kyle didn't go to school, so they could sleep in.

It seemed logical then, that Brian hadn't been part of the other robberies. With a sick feeling, Sammy remembered Kyle's fist threatening Brian on Thursday afternoon. That had to be when they made Brian be part of their gang.

"Don't think about that," she told herself. At the sound of her voice, Jack lifted his head and thumped his tail sleepily. Sammy slid off the chair and crouched down to stroke his silky fur. "Papa Jack said when the going gets tough, the tough get going." Sammy rubbed Jack's ears and he sighed. "Brian needs to get going."

His brothers had filched his money. There was no point in giving him any more – even if she had it. She was sure they would get that too.

"Brian needs someone who can help him," Sammy told Jack. "I don't think it's me."

For a long time, Sammy sat on the floor, stroking Jack, thinking about how she could get help for Brian. Her mom and Erin's parents would probably say it was none of their business. The police would put him in jail. Mrs. Sovich would talk him to death. Mrs. Martinez! The principal would know what to do.

The more Sammy thought about it, the better she liked her plan. Mrs. Martinez could keep the money for Brian. What happened to him *was* her business. Brian said she'd been calling Child Protective Services about him. Sammy quickly pushed the thought from her mind that that hadn't helped Brian so far.

She had a plan, she thought happily. When you have a plan, things work out.

Erin came back at 3:30. Jack stood up and stretched from his nap on the kitchen floor. When he saw Erin, he hurtled at her, barking.

"Down! Sit!" Erin commanded. Jack backed up a few steps and kept on barking. "We're going to the library," she announced. "Jack will be a much happier dog when he learns how to behave."

"I think he's happy now," Sammy shouted over the din. "I gave him a peanut butter sandwich, he napped all afternoon, and now he's terrorizing my friends."

Erin giggled. Jack barked and tried to jump on her. She pushed him down. "You are being a very bad boy," she scolded. "I said, sit!"

Whether he understood the command or temporarily got tired of barking, Jack sat. Sammy felt a quick jab of jealousy.

"Good boy," Erin said. "Should we put him in the basement?"

They tried. For nearly half an hour, they tried. Sammy even threw an entire peanut butter sandwich and a slice of ham downstairs to get Jack into the cellar. He barked defiantly at the open door and ran around the house wildly. He would not go down.

"Okay, stay upstairs then!" Sammy declared. "You are such a bad dog I don't even know why I have you!"

Jack crouched down, barking furiously at her.

Close to tears, Sammy slammed shut the doors of all the rooms. "Let's go," she said to Erin. "I'll just leave him out."

"What about your Mom?"

"Do you see her here? She'll talk to her friends until dinnertime. Besides, I don't care."

When they left the house, Sammy slammed that door too. When she glanced back, Jack was looking out the window, still barking. Once on her bike, she pedaled hard up the hill, leaving Erin behind. Would Jack ever be a nice dog like Casey?

At the Library, Erin once again took charge. They headed straight for the computers and typed "dog training" into the subject prompt. A long list of titles popped up. Erin efficiently wrote down the Dewey Decimal number.

"Aren't you going to list the books?" Sammy asked.

Erin shook her head. "There's lots of them. Now that we know where they are, we can pick out the best ones."

It was fun. They sat on the carpet with the books, exclaiming over weird breeds of dogs and trying to pick the best book for training Jack. Sammy found one about training aggressive dogs, but Erin liked one with a lot of pictures of a dog that looked like Casey.

"Jack will be a great dog," she said. "You just have to follow the directions."

"I don't think it's like making cookies," Sammy argued. "Jack's going to break all the rules."

"If you think that way, he doesn't have a hope," Erin said. "It's like raising a baby. You have to be patient and kind and never forget you're the boss."

"Yeah, like we've raised so many babies," Sammy retorted.

Erin giggled. "Well, it sounds good, doesn't it?"

Sammy rolled her eyes and then giggled too. Arm in arm they high stepped out of the library, singing *"How much is the doggie in the window?"* When they saw one of the boys in their class drive by, they stopped abruptly and then practically fell over laughing.

It was like before, Sammy decided, as she wiped her streaming eyes. Before all the bad stuff happened and she never thought about anything much but doing her homework and playing with Erin.

Like a quick shot of sunshine, she wondered if maybe things could feel like that again.

"Race you!" she took off on her bike. Erin shrieked and laughed behind her.

She really loved the feel of the cold air in her mouth and the wind streaming through her hair. Things would feel good again.

Good, however, was not what was waiting at home.

Sammy waved good-bye to Erin at the corner and then pedaled home in a blissful cloud of expectations. But, as soon as she opened the kitchen door, she knew the good times were over.

Her mother was slamming dishes into the sink. Chewed up chunks of paper littered the floor. In the basement, Jack was throwing himself against the closed cellar door.

When Sammy walked in, her mother turned to her. "Nice of you to show up," she snapped. "And I really appreciate the way you left that animal loose." She held up her arm. There was a long tear in her silk shirt. "This was my one and only new shirt. I thought, hey, if I'm going to have a one woman show, then I should dress the part." She slammed another pan into the sink. "Of course, it was probably a stupid idea anyway, so why would I need a silk shirt? But we all dream."

"I'm sorry," Sammy managed.

"So am I," Linda Connor went on. "Randy offered me a job as an instructor at the college."

"A job! That's great!"

"Yeah, right. Introduction to Ceramics! Six hours a day. Kids who need an easy class and housewives looking for something to do."

"Oh," Sammy said. "Can't you do your pottery the rest of the time?"

"In the leftover bits of evenings?" She folded her arms and leaned against the counter. "Pathetic, aren't I? Randy said I'm not quite ready for a show. I knew I could never be as smart or as organized or as successful as Dad. But I didn't think I'd be a complete failure."

Sammy didn't know what to say. "I don't think you're a failure."

"Oh, yeah? That's why you got a job, isn't it? Because you didn't think I would even be able to buy groceries!"

"It was because of Jack," Sammy protested. "I had to be responsible for him. Papa Jack said it's important to be responsible."

"Papa Jack wasn't always right, you know! He wasn't right about me!" She stood up straight. "Or maybe he was. Your dog chewed up my contract. So, I guess I can't take that job now, even if I want to. That's life for you."

She stalked out of the kitchen. Not knowing what else to do, Sammy picked up the fragments of paper and smoothed them out. One by one, she piled them on the table. There were two copies, one already signed by the college. It would have been a job for her mother. It would have looked after everything, but Jack chewed it up.

Wham! He slammed against the door again.

Furious, Sammy pounded her fist against the door. "You stupid dog! You ruined everything! Don't you have any sense? Can't you do anything right! You...you devil!"

She threw her books on the table and ignoring Jack's barking and howling, ran to her bedroom. She yanked the covers over herself and nested into their warmth.

Why was it that when she tried so hard, things kept going so wrong?

Susan Brown

Chapter 17

It Isn't Easy

Around dinnertime, Sammy roused herself to take Jack out of the cellar. He didn't seem to know or care how bad he'd been. When she opened the cellar door, he came prancing out, tail wagging.

Sammy silently snapped on his leash. He mouthed her wrist nervously, but didn't bite down.

"Come on," she grunted.

They went down to the creek. It was a wild place hidden in the middle of the subdivision – salmon ran up it in the spring, so it had been spared the bulldozer. Ducking under the drooping branches of a huge hemlock, Sammy and Jack plunged into the cool green shadows of the creek bank. Jack joyfully scampered between rocks and bushes, darting now and then into the rushing water. Sammy followed along the trail.

They skirted a moldy mattress and a pile of old beer cans and headed upstream. Moss grew emerald green on the rocks and rotting tree stumps. Sweeps of pine and fir branches dipped in the breeze. The last rays of the sun dappled over rocks and stream and rustled the leaves of vine maples.

Every few minutes Jack would veer back to brush Sammy's legs with his damp shoulder. "Checking to make sure I'm still here?" she asked. "C'm'ere, boy."

He ignored her again.

"It's getting late," Sammy said. "We'd better go back."

She gave a tug on the leash. Jack strained in the opposite direction. Sammy yanked harder. Jack whirled and stood facing her, head lowered, growling angrily at her.

Suddenly, that was too much. Sammy threw down the leash. "Okay, have it your own way. I'm doing my best, but you don't care! You just get me in trouble and then you bark at me. If you don't want to come, then don't! Get lost! Get run over or something. If you don't want to be with me, I don't care!"

She turned on her heel and scrambled up a stony bank to the path. Before she reached it, Jack was in front of her, barking, blocking her way.

"Go away!" Sammy yelled. "Can't you see I don't want you any more! You're too much trouble."

She pushed past him, leg banging his shoulder.

"*Ooowww...*" The howl was soft, hardly more then a whine.

Sammy turned around. Jack crouched down, front paws extended, like he was pleading with her. His brown eyes looked as if they would shed tears if they could.

Rubbing her own eyes, Sammy stooped down and grabbed the end of the leash. Jack bumped against her then, weaving back and forth so his sides and shoulders brushed her legs over and over. She knelt down and put her arms around his neck. "I didn't mean it," she whispered. "I love you, Jack. I didn't mean it."

He licked her cheek and trotted beside her all the way back to the house.

The next day, Sunday, when Sammy and her mother met in the hallway or kitchen, they were as polite as two strangers.

"I have a lot of work to do," her mom said. "Would you like anything special for dinner? I'll start it before I go into my studio."

"No, that's okay," Sammy replied. "Anything's fine. I'll make something so you don't have to break your concentration."

Like we don't know each other, Sammy thought. Like we've dropped the leash and said do whatever you want.

Sammy spent a lot of the day in the yard with Jack. She read the books about dog training and then tried to train her puppy. After a while she started reading the text out loud to him.

"Listen to this," she said. "It says here that, 'Dogs wag their tails when they are happy....' Are you happy, Jack?" The pup's tail waved in the air. "Good. Because it says that training should be fun for the dog. It doesn't say anything about being fun for me. That's not fair....Okay, it says I should say 'Come' when you're coming anyway. So you come, and I'll say the right word."

Jack barked, took the leash in his mouth and tugged.

Sammy laughed. "No, I don't come to you. You come to me! Don't you get it?" Jack yanked the leash again. "I guess not."

Giving up, she dropped down on the grass. Jack trotted over and sat on her. "Yeouff! You're squishing me!" Sammy threw her arms around his neck. He shoved his nose into her ear, licked once and then panted happily.

Sammy smoothed the thick fur over Jack's shoulders, feeling the softness and the strong muscles underneath. "You've got to be a good dog, Jack," she whispered. "Mom is so mad at you. You've got to show her how good you can be. You don't want to end up at the Humane Society or something, do you?"

Jack gave no indication that he was listening.

Sammy thought about the chewed up contract. Did they only give it out once, and if you didn't bring it back they hired someone else? She didn't know. All she knew was her mother was furious with Jack – again. And she, Sammy, hadn't gotten very far with helping out Brian either.

"I've blown everything," she said. "But I'm not going to let it stay that way. I'm going to tell you what I'm thinking about, Jack. You just bark if you think it's a good idea, okay?"

The puppy spotted a squirrel and leaped off her lap. Sammy sighed. "You know, you make a lousy listener." She stood up and twitched Jack's leash. "C'mon boy, let's go in."

As usual, he ignored her.

Sammy took a deep breath. She had thought and thought. Her plan to help Brian could work. It didn't matter that everything else was going wrong. Lifting her head,

Sammy walked into the office and up to the principal's open door.

"Mrs. Martinez," Sammy said. "I have to talk to you."

Mrs. Martinez glanced over from the computer with her warm smile in place. "I'm really busy now, Sammy. Could you...?" She seemed to suddenly see Sammy's face. Her hands dropped from the computer keys to her lap and the smile disappeared. Her face was serious now, but warmer even than it had been with its smile.

"Come in and sit down, Sammy." As Sammy perched on the edge of the chair, Mrs. Martinez shut the office door, and then sat down opposite her, leaning forward. "What do you want to talk about?"

"It's about Brian," Sammy said. "I want to help him...but I don't know how. He's not bad, even though everybody thinks he is. He gave me my dog. He said it was because he didn't want him any more, but I think he did want him. His brothers..." her voice faltered.

"Yes, his brothers," Mrs. Martinez said. "I know all about his brothers."

Sammy nodded. "Brian has to get away. They hurt him and I think they make him do bad things. He's not bad," Sammy repeated. "He's just been hurt a lot and nobody loves him." She thought again about Jack, snarling in fear and anger, then lifting his paw, hoping for a treat. "I have it all worked out. I have to tell you a secret though."

"Okay."

"I said I wouldn't tell, but I think I should." Sammy hoped Mrs. Martinez would tell her she was doing the right thing, but the principal just waited. "Brian told me he's going to run away to stay with his mother. She's in San Francisco. If you help him find out where she is exactly, he could go stay with her, then everything would be fine."

Mrs. Martinez sat back and looked down, but Sammy went on in a rush. "I have a job earning money to pay for my dog. I gave Brian twenty-five dollars on Friday, but his brothers saw and stole it from him. When I get paid next, I could give the money to you, and then we could buy him a bus ticket and he could go there and he'd be okay."

Sammy waited anxiously. Mrs. Martinez frowned and looked down at her clasped hands.

"Sammy, you're a nice girl," she said.

"But I'm being really stupid," Sammy interrupted.

"No," Mrs. Martinez said. "You aren't being stupid at all. I'm going to tell you something

I want you to keep to yourself. I've already located Mrs. Haydon and spoken to her."

Sammy felt a flood of joy spread over her – until she looked at Mrs. Martinez' face.

"Mrs. Haydon doesn't feel she's in a position to look after Brian right now. She's out of work."

Sammy gripped the arms of her chair. "What difference does that make? My mother doesn't have a job. It's really awful not having any money, but that's totally different. Doesn't she want him? She's his mother. She has to want him!"

"Not everyone is good at parenting. It's something you have to learn, and if no one has ever taught you...." Mrs. Martinez' voice got slower and lower. "Mrs. Haydon said she tried for several years, but the boys weren't turning out well. She doesn't feel she can do anything for Brian."

"She could love him." Sammy slumped back, folding her arms tightly against her chest. "She could learn to be a good mother and to do what's right, couldn't she? Then things will work out."

"Not everybody believes that, Sammy."

Sammy jumped out of her chair and paced from one end of the office to the other. She wiped her forearm across her face.

"They should believe it because it's true. My grandfather told me so, and he was always right."

Mrs. Martinez stood up and hugged her. "You're a lucky girl to have had a grandfather like that."

"But he died and I really miss him. Sometimes, I think its okay and then something little reminds me of him and I start to cry. And it's so hard doing the right thing all by myself."

"I know," Mrs. Martinez whispered. "I know. He'd be so proud of you."

Sammy took a deep breath and pulled away. Mrs. Martinez grabbed two tissues from a box – one for each of them.

Sammy sank down on the chair again. "But what about Brian? Who will fix things for him? I know...does he have a grandfather? A nice one maybe?"

Mrs. Martinez put her hands on Sammy's shoulders. "I'll keep trying Sammy. I promise. But it isn't easy."

Sammy nodded. "I know."

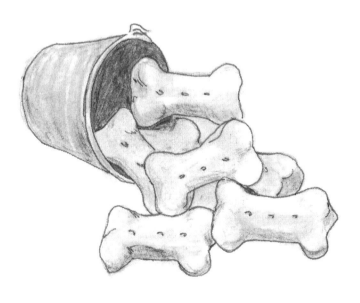

192   Susan Brown

Chapter 18

"He really is a good dog..."

Brian came late to school that morning.

During math, he flung the door open and looked around belligerently. When Mrs. Bennett simply glanced at him with pursed lips, he announced loudly. "Guess, I'm late. Bet I didn't miss anything. Nothing to miss with this bunch of losers."

Sammy held her breath. Game over. Mrs. Bennett would kill him.

But the teacher only said evenly. "Please sit down, Brian. We have a lot of work to cover today. Class," she said in a louder voice, "I want everyone to do some sheets on averaging and estimating. Ashley, please get them from my desk and pass them out."

"Boring!" Brian declared.

Even when the paper was set down in front of her, Sammy kept shifting her eyes from Mrs. Bennett to Brian. Now he was twisting around in his chair, like he couldn't get comfortable.

He took out two pencils and did a drum solo on the edge of his desk.

Mrs. Bennett just ignored him.

Frank started banging a pencil on his desk, too – until Mrs. Bennett gave him the evil eye. Mid-beat, he stopped.

"You made a lot of mistakes in your math homework, Frank," Mrs. Bennett said. "You can't afford to waste in-class work time."

"Sorry," Frank muttered. Like the rest of the class, he bent his head over the work sheets.

"I don't get this," Brian yelled. "This is really dumb and I'm not doing it!"

Mrs. Bennett turned her back to him and said nothing.

Sammy found her palms were sweating and she could hardly think. There wasn't a sound in the classroom except Brian slamming his hands on the desk and shifting papers around.

"I don't get this," he repeated, a little less loudly. "I need some help here."

Mrs. Bennett kept her back to him.

Silence.

"Mrs. Bennett," Brian said finally, "I need some help, please."

She turned around then and went to his desk, leaning over so that her face was on the same level as his. "Where are you having trouble?"

Sammy saw him point to a spot on his paper, and then as Mrs. Bennett explained the work, Brian began writing. She murmured something. He laughed and continued writing. The teacher moved on to another student.

Cold with relief, Sammy turned back to her own work. But it seemed nearly impossible to concentrate. Her conversation with Mrs. Martinez kept swirling around and around in her mind.

How could Brian's mother not want him? How could it be that no one at all could want him? A blur of red across the aisle yanked her attention back to the classroom.

"Yeow!" Frank suddenly yelled. "Mrs. Bennett! Brian hit my face with a rubber band!"

"It was an accident," Brian smirked. "I just had it wrapped around my finger and it slipped. I'm *really* sorry, Frank."

"Mrs. Bennett," Tara said. "I don't like to tell, but Brian aimed it at Frank. I saw him. He has a whole package of rubber bands in his desk." She turned to Brian. "What if you'd hit him in the eye!"

Brian laughed. "I could've played marbles with his eyeballs!" He mimed shooting a marble across his desk. "Whacko!"

"You're sick!" Frank shrilled. He clapped one hand protectively over his cheek.

Mrs. Bennett's nostrils flared. "Brian, you'll have to go down to the office." She pointed to the school's rules hanging over the door. "That was neither safe, respectful, responsible, nor kind."

Brian lurched out of his desk and swaggered across the room. "But it got me out of math!" He called over his shoulder.

As he banged out of the door, the rest of the class shot furtive glances at Mrs. Bennett. The teacher took a long, deep breath and then another. Sammy watched in fascination as she clenched and unclenched her hands. The teacher glanced down and caught Sammy's eye.

"Sammy," she said, "please take Brian's math papers down to the office. I'll write a note for Mrs. Pope. Brian will work on the papers while he waits to see Mrs. Martinez."

Sammy nodded and picked up Brian's papers.

"Score one for Mrs. Bennett," Ethan said in a loud whisper. Everyone around him laughed, tension releasing.

"Focus on your work, Ethan," Mrs. Bennett said. But she was smiling.

In the office, Brian was perched on the bench outside Mrs. Martinez office. He didn't look so defiant or so big.

Sammy handed the note to Mrs. Pope and the math sheets to Brian. "Mrs. Bennett wants you to work on these while you wait."

Brian took them glumly, but without protest. Uncomfortably, Sammy shifted from one foot to the other.

"What?" he demanded.

Sammy shrugged. "Nothing. I thought maybe you'd want to hear how Jack's doing."

Brian gave a noncommittal lift of his shoulders. "He's a good dog."

Sammy thought about the chaos Jack left behind him. "Well, he's going to be a good dog. He kind of needs training though."

"No he doesn't," Brian protested. "Does he sit up and beg for you? I taught him to do that. Took him about ten minutes to learn, he's so smart. And a couple of weeks ago..."

"Brian," Mrs. Pope interrupted sternly. "Mrs. Bennett says you're to do your math. Sammy, you get back to your class now."

"Okay," Sammy said. "See you."

"Yeah," Brian replied. "He really is a good dog...."

"He's a great dog," Sammy agreed.

"Let's go," Mrs. Pope reminded them.

Brian nodded and stared at the floor, gently swinging his papers between his knees.

Sammy slowly headed back to class.

Mrs. Betancourt had been wide-awake when Sammy came to read to her that afternoon. She also had a new book ready in her hand.

"So you remembered to come," she said in her slurry voice.

"Of course I did," Sammy didn't know if the indignation sounded in her words.

The old lady chuckled. "You remind me of me at your age," she said. Sammy was appalled. Could she ever become this old and sick?

"Didn't look like you, of course. I had red hair...like fire they all said. But I was busy... busy with important things all the time."

Sammy knew what was coming. "But you found out they weren't so important when you grew up."

Mrs. Betancourt slowly shook her head. "No, child, I found out they were more important."

"I don't get it."

Mrs. Betancourt half smiled and held out her book in a shaky hand. "Here, Darlene marked the poems I want you to read to me...."

The house was silent when Sammy got home that evening. There was no light or movement in the studio. There was no whining and thudding behind the cellar door.

"Jack!" Sammy cried. The door to the basement stood open. She tore through the house, shouting her dog's name.

Silence.

She flung open the back door and ran into the yard. "Jack!" she yelled. "Here boy! Come on, boy! Come on, Jack!"

She waited. And then she heard it. A distant bark...a crescendo of yelps.

Jack!

Sammy raced to the front yard, to the sidewalk. She could hear Jack more clearly now. "I'm coming," she yelled. "Jack! Where are you!"

From the direction of the creek. The sounds were coming from the creek. Sammy tore down the sidewalk. She could hear Jack's barking plainly now. "Here boy!" Sammy yelled. "Here, Jack!"

And then he was racing toward her. Barking and leaping up on her, tongue slathering his joy. Muddy feet planted on her stomach as he rapturously reached up his muzzle up to lick her face. Leash trailing...

Leash...

Sammy grabbed the leather loop and tried to push Jack down. She looked apprehensively down the sidewalk toward the creek. Hands jammed in her pockets, her mother was striding toward her.

She didn't look happy.

"Uh oh," Sammy said softly. "Jack, I think we blew it." Jack plunked down on the pavement beside her. "Hi Mom!" Sammy called.

Her mother gave her the same kind of look Mrs. Bennett had given Frank earlier. Evil eye. "I made the mistake of taking your dog for a walk. Why were you shouting for him like that? He practically broke my arm getting away!"

"I came home," Sammy tried to explain. "No one was there. And Jack was gone and I thought he was lost or maybe...maybe you'd gotten rid of him..." her voice trailed off.

"I ought to," her mother snapped. "And you wouldn't be far behind."

Sammy felt the world going to ice....Didn't her mother want her either?

"What were you thinking?" Linda Connor raged on. "Sammy, what is the matter with you these days?"

"Nothing," Sammy whispered. "Nothing is going on. I don't mean to be so much trouble. I won't be trouble any more. Neither will Jack.

I'll make sure, Mom. I promise. It'll be okay. I promise it will."

Her mother stopped mid-stride and looked back at her. "It better be. What else is going on? Because I'm really sick of your carryings on, you know."

Sammy nodded. "I know. There's nothing else. I just...I guess I just over-reacted because I thought Jack was gone. I didn't know...." She started walking, head down toward the house. Her mother fell into step beside her.

"I know." Her mother snapped. "You thought I'd get rid of him while you were away at school – not even tell you about it. Just let you come home and find your pet had gone," she said bitterly. "Maybe tell you he ran away so that you wouldn't even think to be mad at me."

Confused, Sammy looked up at her. "But it would be easier for you that way," she said. She turned in toward their driveway, but her mother had stopped.

"Yes," she said. "It would be easier for me."

202   Susan Brown

Chapter 19

Trust

They walked down the driveway in cold silence. Even Jack had lost some bounce.

"I've got some bowls to fire." Her mom headed straight back to the studio, leaving Sammy standing beside the porch with Jack.

Instead of going in, Sammy plunked down in the grass and leaned against the wooden wall.

What had made Brian's mom leave? Her own dad had left before she was born. But he'd been seventeen like her mom, so when his folks up and moved he'd gone too. But she and her mom had Papa Jack so they didn't need him at all.

Jack nuzzled her, his tongue moving over the bit of cheek he could reach.

Sammy unclasped her knees and put her arms around his neck. "You've got to be good," she whispered. "You've got to learn to be good. Do you hear that, Jack?"

The dog twisted away, and then spotting a squirrel, started barking.

Sammy grabbed the neck fur on either side of his head with both fists. "Listen to me!" she shouted. "Listen to me, you stupid dog!"

Jack whined and tugged, but she didn't let go.

"I've lost Papa Jack and I'm not going to lose my mother because of you. Do you understand that? Do you understand?"

Jack whined again. He ducked his head. Sammy wanted to hit him, clout him on the head like Brian had. She just wanted to love Jack. Was he going to chase away her mother?

"Stop it," Sammy told herself. "Mom isn't going to leave...she's got the studio here...and the house..."

Sammy tugged at the leash and Jack obediently followed her through the kitchen door at the back of the house. She unsnapped the leash and looked around. Dishes were piled in the sink and the floor was being patterned by Jack's muddy paws.

"Stay still," Sammy ordered the dog as she tried to wipe him clean with an old dishtowel. He pulled back hard, nearly tipping her over, but she rubbed off most of the mud. Jack flopped down then, and began licking his own paws.

Next, Sammy poured cleaning detergent and hot water into the bucket. Then she let the water run over the dishes in the sink. They could soak while she washed the floor.

As she swished the mop across the floor, she bumped the swinging door into the living room. It came loose from its catch and swung shut, crashing into her shoulder as it went.

"Ow!"

She tried to make it stay back against the wall, but she didn't seem to have the trick of making it catch. It kept swinging shut on them, once booting Jack on the behind. He looked so startled and indignant, that Sammy had to laugh.

"Don't worry. I'll fix it."

Sammy leaned the mop against the counter and went into the yard. It took about two seconds to find a big enough rock.

"Someone must have found this at the ocean," she told Jack. The stone was about six inches across, smooth as an egg, with rings of paler rock exposed by the eons of erosion. "Beautiful," Sammy murmured. When she put it on the floor to hold back the door, the pale grey of the rock nearly matched the pale grey pattern of the tile.

"A decorator touch," Sammy told Jack. She picked up the mop again.

It didn't take long to finish the kitchen floor, so Sammy kept going, doing the bathroom floor and any other tiled surface she could find. She mopped the landing to the cellar, but not the steps. It was getting dark and the basement looked spooky.

She shivered. "Did you see any ghosts down there, Jack?" she asked.

He pricked up his ears.

"No wonder you don't want to go down there at night." Sammy backed out and shut the door. "I've got to tell you Jack, you're being very good. You keep that up, okay?"

Jack's tail thumped twice.

Next Sammy started on the dishes. She didn't mind the feel of the hot soap bubbles sliding through her hands. Happily, she poofed a couple into the air. They'd had a dishwasher at the other house, but Papa Jack had sometimes filled the sink and done a few dishes by hand anyway.

She remembered how she'd stand on a stool – she must've been a lot younger, and talk to him while he washed up the dishes. His hands were brown from working in his rose garden. She remembered seeing one small soap bubble slide across the face of his ring. It glided slowly on the smooth black stone and stuck on the small diamond in the corner.

Then it popped.

Sammy laid the last dish on the drainer and rinsed out the sink.

Maybe she should make dinner too. That way, her mom could never think things were bad around here, could she?

Sammy checked out the fridge and freezer. There was a lot of food still, but she didn't really know how to cook most of it. When her stomach growled, she hastily picked up a bag of frozen hash browns.

"I'll put eggs on it and that should be okay, right Jack?" Once again Jack sleepily thumped his tail.

She dropped a half a stick of butter in the old cast iron frying pan that had belonged to Papa Jack's mother, and then turned up the heat. When the butter was melted and hissing, Sammy dropped the hash browns on top of that. She laid on the salt and pepper, waited a couple of minutes then flipped over the potatoes. Jack was circling around her feet now, and whining like he hadn't eaten for a week. Obviously too weak to keep going, he plopped down with his back to the stove and his head ready to rest on her feet.

"You are such a liar, Jack!" Sammy told him.

He whimpered.

She flipped the potatoes again, and then got the eggs from the fridge. She's just cracked the last one over the hash browns when her mom came in.

Linda Connor's eyebrows shot up. "Peace offering?"

Sammy shrugged feeling her face heat up. "I washed the floor and the dishes," she said, worried her mom wouldn't notice.

"So I see." Her mom smiled. "Thank you."

Sammy shrugged again. "No big deal."

While her mom showered, Sammy laid the plates and cutlery on the table. She wished suddenly that she'd thought to go get some flowers or something to put in the center. "Probably too late for flowers anyway," she told Jack.

Next year she'd get some flower seeds for the front of the house. She wished that they'd dug up Papa Jack's roses and brought them to this house.

Sammy pressed her lips together. That was done with. She had to get dinner on the table. She had to make sure her mom didn't think things were too bad.

"Smells great," her mom said, coming back into the kitchen.

Sammy ventured a smile. "I broke one of the egg yolks."

Her mom really smiled then. "Uh oh."

"Mo...om!"

They laughed together. Not because it was funny, but because they were so relieved. Because they were together. They hadn't laughed together for a long time.

"Here," Sammy said. She wrapped the dishtowel around the handle of the pan and carried it over to the table. The hash browns slid onto the plates, almost perfect.

When her Mom put the first forkful in her mouth, she closed her eyes a moment then made an "O" with her lips and puffed out steam. "Hot!" she cried.

Jack came over and slid his head into her lap, lifting his nose only slightly to sniff the aromas.

"He's getting so tame," Sammy said. "Isn't he getting tame?"

"Sure," her mother snorted, pushing his head from her lap. "While there's food. The rest of the time he's right up there with a Tasmanian devil. They make about the same kind of pet, I believe."

Sammy had a sudden memory of being at the beach with Papa Jack. He had built a kite out of wooden doweling and brown paper that was even taller than he was. In the strong ocean wind, he had set it loose. It had torn into the sky, dipping and weaving – not like any kite Sammy had ever seen.

"Just like a...what do you call those things...a Tasmanian devil," Papa had said. The kite crashed down then, swooping as though attacking them. They'd had to dive out of the way. The paper had torn. After Papa mended it, they drew an evil-eyed monster on the paper – their own Tasmanian devil.

Sammy looked over at Jack, sitting hopefully by the table. "He isn't wild," she insisted. "And how's he going to get tame when we lock him in the cellar every night. When you love someone, you trust them."

"Sure."

"Well, isn't that true?" Sammy insisted.

"No, it isn't," her mother said. "Trusting someone doesn't make them trustworthy. You already know that. You didn't trust me this afternoon. You thought I'd given Jack away without saying anything to you."

"It wasn't like that," Sammy muttered.

"It was exactly like that," her Mom said. She stood up. "That was a great meal, Sammy. I'm going to check my email, and then I'll clean up the kitchen. Please get Jack in the cellar as soon as he's eaten."

"Mom..."

Her mother shook her head. "It's late, sweetheart. We both need to get to bed." She put her plate in the sink then headed toward her bedroom.

Sammy sat where she was, stroking Jack's silky head. Then with a sigh, she got up and put her own plate in the sink.

"Come on, Jack," she said. "It's time to go to bed."

She pulled open the cellar door and scooted him down the dark stairs.

212   Susan Brown

Chapter 20

Don't Hurt Her!

Sammy lay in bed, hands clasped behind her head, watching the moon creep across the pictures on her wall.

Her mom was wrong. Jack shouldn't be locked in the cellar every night. With a knife-like sense of panic, Sammy reviewed her plan to prove to her mother that Jack was a good dog, a *trustworthy* dog. That neither of them were troublesome. Things weren't *too* bad. They weren't like Brian and his brothers.

How could Jack show what a good dog he is, shut up like that? He should be up on the bed beside her, warm body heavy against her legs. She imagined his soft, deep breathing and the quick lick his tongue would plant on her cheek. She shouldn't have to be so alone. No dog, no Papa Jack. And her mother...

Bang!!

She jumped and held her breath. What was that sound? Not Jack – the noise came from outside. Maybe a raccoon trying to get at the garbage.

She glanced at the clock on her nightstand. Twelve forty-eight. Her mom had to be asleep by now. It was only eight-thirty when she'd sent Sammy off to bed. Rebelliously, Sammy had crawled under the blankets, still dressed, and read by flashlight under the covers. The rest of the evening, she could hear her mom pacing around in the kitchen, brewing coffee, and then making two or three phone calls.

Sammy pushed back the covers and quietly slipped out of bed. Careful to avoid any squeaky boards she eased her way into the hall. A cold breeze iced her feet.

Weird. Mom didn't usually leave the windows open.

She stopped and listened. For a second she thought she heard her mom in the living room. But no, Sammy could see the sleeping form of her mother through the partly open bedroom door. It must be that breeze from the open window.

From behind the cellar door Jack barked sharply. Once...then again, with rising insistence.

"No!" Sammy dashed down the hall – she had to get him quiet before he woke up her mom.

Then she saw them – three figures leaning over the television. She skidded to a stop, froze. She opened her mouth. Funny. She didn't seem to be able to make a sound.

In the background, Jack's voice rose louder and louder.

The three intruders twisted and stared at her. She stared at them. Like a TV show. All dressed in black with black ski masks over their faces. Not human.

"Get her!" the tallest one growled.

"Mom!" Sammy screamed. She tried to run. One of the thieves leaped across the room and grabbed her arm. "Mom! Call the poli…"

He slapped a gloved hand over her face. She was choking. Desperate she kicked, twisted, bit down hard.

"Ow!" Her captor swore.

She twisted free. Noise. Make noise!

She screamed and ran around the living room, dodging, crying.

Her mother, in crumpled pajamas, staggered barefooted out from the bedroom. "Sammy!" she cried.

Jack howled and barked and hurled himself against the cellar door in the kitchen.

Sammy twisted at her mom's voice. Mistake. The biggest one grabbed her, twisting her arm up behind. Sammy cried out sharply.

"Leave her alone!" One of the thieves yelled.

"Brian?" Sammy knew the voice. She squirmed to look up at her captor. Joe. It was Joe. He looked down through the slits in his ski mask and viciously forced her arm farther up her back.

"Ow...no!" Sammy cried out.

"Let her go!" her mother ran forward a few steps then abruptly stopped.

Click.

A long knife blade flashed in front of Sammy's face. The room became very still. The only sounds were the heavy breathing of five people staring at each other and the muffled cacophony of Jack's frantic attempts to escape.

Kyle giggled. "We got you good now!"

Joe twisted Sammy's arm tighter. She cried out.

"Don't hurt her." Linda Connor's voice was low, insistent. "What do you want?"

"Money, jewelry, credit cards. Now." Joe's voice was high pitched.

"Joe, they don't have anything hardly. Let's go," Brian pleaded.

"Shut up!" his brother hissed. "Move it, lady."

Sammy's mother stood very still. "You can have everything. Just don't hurt my daughter," she repeated.

"Maybe. Maybe not." Joe laughed. His voice sounded really weird. Drugs, Sammy thought. Erin said he did drugs, big time...

Her mother said in the same even voice. "Sammy, stay very still. I'm going to get them everything they want. So you just stay there, sweetheart."

"Make it fast!" Joe waved the knife again.

"My purse is over by the chair," Linda Connor gestured to it. "It has two credit cards but only three dollars in it. I keep the rest of my cash in a cookie jar in the kitchen. I'll get it."

Sammy held her breath. There was no money in the kitchen. Her mom wouldn't leave her, would she?

"Mom," she cried softly.

"It's okay, baby," her mom soothed. "I'll be right back."

She walked toward the kitchen. Kyle grabbed the handbag and tore it open. He yanked out the three bills and fumbled for the cards. Behind his ski mask, Brian made little noises, like an argument he was afraid to say. Sammy stared transfixed at the knife that was slowly lowering.

"Joe," Brian's voice finally came out barely louder than a whisper. "I don't want to do this. It's a bad idea. Let's just go before the cops show up or something...."

"Cops?" Kyle looked at Joe stupidly. "Do you think she has a cell phone?"

"Hey!" Joe shouted. He jerked around, loosening his hold.

Sammy yanked away and raced for the kitchen. Joe lumbered after her. The back door was open. Where was her mother?

Joe grabbed her shoulder from behind. Hard fingers clawed her as she twisted and fought. Her foot hit something hard and she stumbled forward, out of Joe's reach.

From the corner of her eye, she saw the heavy swinging door wham outward, catching Joe, knocking him back into the living room.

Linda Connor leapt from her hiding place between the wall and door.

"Get out, Sammy!" she screamed. "Run!"

Joe slammed through the swinging door, whamming it back against the wall. Linda Connor grabbed the broom and held it like a shield in front of them, warding off Joe.

"Get out, Sammy. Now!"

Sobbing, Sammy fled out the open back door, into the night. She stopped, shifting form one foot to another.

"Mom!" She couldn't leave her mother.

Inside, Joe laughed a funny laugh and twisted his knife so that the scant light flashed on its blade. Sammy's mom raised the broom, staring Joe straight in the eyes.

"Get out of my house, you little creep."

Kyle crowded in behind Joe. His hand was clamped on Brian's arm. "He tried to run out on us!"

"We'll get him later." Joe stepped toward Linda Connor. "First things first."

Frozen with fear, Sammy watched from the shadows outside. She wouldn't leave her mom.

Wham! Jack howled and threw himself against the cellar door.

"Jack!" she whispered.

Joe raised his knife. Sammy tore back into the kitchen and threw open the cellar door.

Like a black demon, Jack hurtled out. He pressed himself briefly against Linda Connor's leg, and then stepped forward. The snarl started low in his throat. Teeth glinted. Head lowered. The growl slowly filled the kitchen.

Joe's hand trembled. He licked his lips. Kyle stepped back and tripped over the rock that had held the door, bringing Brian down on top of him. He clawed his way toward the living room.

"Get him, Jack," Brian whispered. He rolled and scrambled into the living room, too.

Jack took one step forward toward Joe, then another.

"Get back, you stupid mutt!" Joe shrilled. He raised his knife higher.

Jack's ears flattened and his fangs shone in the half light.

"I said down!" Joe slashed out. Jack lunged.

"Jack!" Sammy screamed.

Crack!

Her mother slammed the broom down on Joe's arm. The blade missed. The dog's fangs ripped a swath from Joe's shirt. Jack lunged again. Joe twisted, stabbed.

The puppy yelped and fell back. Joe's hysterical giggle was choked off when Jack twisted around again and with a snarl, shot forward.

Linda Connor hurled the broom at Joe, grabbed Sammy in her arms and ran through the back door into the night.

Savage barking crescendoed. Joe screamed.

"Mom! I can't leave him! I have to save Jack!" Sammy fought against her mother's grip, struggling to get back.

Her mother didn't answer, just pulled her at a dead run toward the road. They reached the end of the driveway, just as the police cars silently shot over the crest of the hill.

Chapter 21

Saving Jack

Barefoot, Sammy and her mother watched from the road as the police pulled into the driveway, blocked the road, and guns drawn, stole up to the house.

"Mom, we have to get Jack," Sammy begged. "We have to save him!"

Her mother shook her head. "The police will take care of him."

"Mom, we can't leave him!" Sammy pulled and wriggled, but her Mom held her arm tightly. "What if Joe hurt him!"

Her mother pulled her into a tight hug. "I won't let anyone hurt you, baby. No one."

The front door opened and Brian tore outside, pursued by Kyle. The police simply grabbed them and slammed them against cars to be searched for weapons. The ski masks were pulled off as the boys were handcuffed.

"Oh, Brian," Sammy said softly. Her classmate's face was contorted with fear and despair. His eyes were wild, like Jack's had been.

Sammy broke from her mother and ran forward. "Brian," she yelled.

He looked at her startled, like he was surprised she was there. Blue and white lights strobed over his face.

"It'll be okay," she said.

Brian shook his head and started to cry silently.

"I'll...I'll look after everything," Sammy said.

"You can't," Brian said.

"But somebody can. You've got to ask for help....and....you've got your father and Mrs. Martinez and Mrs. Bennett and..."

"In you go, son." The police officer opened the door and steered Brian into the barred back seat. "Watch your head." The door slammed and locked. They put Kyle in another car.

Sammy tried again to dart toward the house, but an officer caught her. Someone dropped a blanket over Sammy's shoulders. She hadn't been aware before that she was shaking. The blue and white lights flashed weirdly over their house and the dark trees. The static echo of the police radio broke the night quiet. A few neighbors were gathering in the driveway. A uniformed officer was setting out portable floodlights.

Aid cars screamed up and the Medics ran into the house.

Sammy's mom left the policewoman she was giving information to, and came over to Sammy.

"Oh, baby, are you okay?"

The officer let go of her. Sammy buried her face in her mom's shoulder and sobbed.

A few minutes later the police escorted Joe out of the house. There was blood on his ripped shirt and Medics had wrapped bandages around his shoulder and neck. He was swearing loudly. The police officer ignored him as though he was not worth the trouble of hearing.

Sammy's mom hugged her tightly and stared as the teen was thrust into the police car. "Good riddance," she said.

Sammy raised her head to watch them drive away. "Mom, please! What about Jack?"

"Let's go!" she agreed.

They raced toward the back door and pushed it open.

There was a lot of blood – in drips and splatters and puddles. Jack lay on the kitchen floor, head at an awful angle.

"Oh Jack," Sammy whispered. A policeman was pressing a dishtowel firmly against the slash across Jack's chest.

"Is he...?" Linda Connor asked.

The policeman looked up. "Your dog's hurt pretty bad, Ma'am. You better get him to a vet real quick."

Sammy dropped down beside Jack. His white ruff was streaked with browning red. His eyes were half open. "Oh, Jack," she breathed.

"Hold this pad," the policeman moved her hand to the bloody towel. "Good and tight now. You okay?"

Sammy nodded. He grabbed another towel, folded it and laid it over the first one.

Her mom disappeared and returned with towels, a pillowcase and a blanket. She knelt down beside them. "Sammy hold his head and muzzle. If you don't mind, officer."

The policeman held the pad. Sammy wrapped her arm over Jack's head and then put her hand over his mouth. "It's okay, Jack," Sammy crooned. "Mom?"

"Just hold him," her mom said. "Good boy, Jack, just hang in there..."

Quickly she made a new dressing of the clean towel, and with the policeman's help, knotted it around Jack's chest with strips torn from the pillowcase. Weakly, Jack tried to lift his head. He whimpered.

"Mom...you're hurting him!"

"I have to make it tight. We've got to get the bleeding stopped." Jack's tail lifted and flopped down again. Then she wrapped the blanket around him so that only his head showed. He kicked weakly in the blanket then lay still.

"Sammy get my jacket and purse," she said quietly. "Could you give me a hand," she asked the policeman. He nodded. Sammy ran for the purse and coat.

They carried Jack to the car. Sammy sat in the back, holding Jack so that he wouldn't slide off the seat. He wasn't moving now.

A policeman came to the window. "Mrs. Connor, we have a few more questions."

"Later," Linda Connor said. "I have to get my dog to the vet."

Before he could reply, she put her car in gear, and backed out onto the street. "Now we put it to the floor," she told Sammy.

When the car wheeled down the road, Jack opened his eyes again. "Good boy, Jack," Sammy whispered. Under the blanket, Sammy could see his tail thump. She leaned over close to his face, and his hot tongue swiped her cheek.

It seemed to take forever but the clock on the dashboard showed only seven minutes passed. Sammy was sure her mother broke all the speed limits, except on the turns. Then she'd slowed down so the car didn't jerk.

Jack wasn't moving at all when they carried him into the emergency vet's office.

"Hey!" Linda Connor shouted. "Please! We've got an emergency here!"

A young woman in a white coat stuck her head out the office door. "Yes?" She did a double take at Linda Connor's pajamas and the blood smearing them.

"Our dog was attacked. He's been slashed with a knife."

"Doctor Sprague! We need you!" the woman called. She didn't wait for the vet. In a flash she was around the corner, her arms under Jack's heavy body. "Oh, poor baby," she crooned. "In here."

They took Jack into the small room and laid him on a table. She had already started unknotting the sheet when the vet hurried in – a big man with a long ponytail.

"It's a knife wound," Sammy's mother said.

The vet nodded and worked alongside his assistant. Sammy leaned against the wall trying to breath.

"Ouch!" the vet exclaimed softly when the wound was laid bare. He laid a stethoscope against Jack's chest. "Heartbeat's slow but it's strong," he murmured. "Your bandaging saved him from bleeding to death. What happened?"

Sammy's mom told them briefly.

"Oh, good dog," Dr. Sprague said. Jack tried to twist away then, but the vet gently held him. "We're going to have to put you to sleep for a while..."

"No!" Sammy and her mom cried together.

"Anesthesia," Dr. Sprague said, "so he won't hurt himself while we stitch him up."

Sammy clung to her mom's hand while the vet and his assistant put a cone over Jack's face. Within seconds he was lying limply. They put a breathing tube down his throat which made Sammy want to cry again.

The vet checked Jack's gums. "Nice and pink...he's doing fine."

They shaved his chest around the slash, and with a syringe flushed out the dried blood and hair. Then they poured a blue liquid all over the cut."

"Will that hurt?" Sammy asked.

"Not at all," Dr. Sprague said. "This kills all the bacteria."

"Will he be okay?" Sammy tried not to let her voice quiver.

"I think so...I'll stitch him up now, and we'll see how he's doing. You can get some coffee or hot chocolate out front if you want."

They went into the waiting room then and sat on the stiff sofa together. Sammy chewed on her finger. Her mom simply sat.

As Sammy stared at the night window, she saw Brian's face again and again. At the same time, like an overlay, she saw his eager pride when he'd talked about the tricks he had taught Jack.

"Mom," she said, "what's going to happen to Brian?"

Her mom shrugged. "I don't know. A lot, I hope."

"But, Mom, he's not bad. He's like Jack. Nobody's ever loved him and his brothers hurt him. Somebody has to help!"

"Maybe this will smarten him up, and he'll help himself." Her mom straightened in her chair.

"Mrs. Martinez tried to help," Sammy said. "Maybe his Dad didn't know what was happening to Brian. He came to school when Brian was in trouble..." Sammy paused, then blurted out, "Mom, I told him I would fix everything, but I can't."

Her mom shook her head. "No, baby. When it comes right down to it, people have to fix themselves. Papa Jack would be proud of you. For the way you tried." She squeezed her hand. "I'm proud of you, too."

After a while the assistant came back out and sat at the desk. "He's doing fine," she told them. "I'll make up your bill now. You can pay this part now, or the whole thing when you pick up Jack tomorrow."

Sammy felt a new surge of fear.

"Mom?" she whispered. "I don't get paid for at least another week."

Red crept up her mother's neck. "Don't worry, baby. We can cover it with what's left in the savings."

"And then what?" Sammy's chest seemed to be constricting.

"I'm starting work at the college on Monday," she said.

"What? But I thought...."

Her mother shrugged. "I...um...called Randy and told him I'd decided the job would be a good thing – give me stability while I experimented with new pottery techniques."

"But what about the contract?"

"I told him the dog chewed it up." She smiled ruefully. "He'll have a new one waiting for me when I go in on Monday. It'll be two weeks before I get my first paycheck. We'll just have to be careful until then."

Sammy grinned. "You know," she said. "I could get us some great sandwiches out of the trash at school – still wrapped even!"

Her mom laughed. "Don't even think about it."

The next night, Sammy lay in the dark. The moon shot beams of silver light through the blinds, highlighting faces and features and bits and pieces of the collage on her wall. In the corner, Jack lay curled in a ball, his elegant tail drawn over his face like a veil.

Sammy twisted over to watch him. She could just see the white edge of the bandage blending into the gleaming white fur. He looked so alone.

She didn't care that the vet had cautioned her that a half-wild dog like Jack would hole up when hurt, that he would snap at anyone who came near him – because that was his instinct.

"It's my instinct to be with you," Sammy whispered. She swung out of bed, wincing at the cold boards under her feet. Wrapping a quilt around herself, Sammy sank down on the floor right beside Jack.

"I'm here," she whispered. "I'll be with you, always, because I love you."

The dog's tail stirred. Jack sighed, moved a little, and then settled into soft breathing again. Sammy sat quietly drowsing. Her hand crept closer to Jack so that it rested against his leg. It wasn't a pat, just a touch of warmth so that he would know she was there.

She didn't know how much later it was, when the door opened. Her mom slipped into the room.

"Aren't you cold, Sammy?" she said softly. "You should be in bed."

Sammy shook her head. "Jack needs me. Nobody should be alone when they're hurt."

Her mom pulled a blanket off the bed, wrapped it around herself and sat down beside her daughter. "Nobody should ever be alone," she agreed softly. "I love you Sammy. I love you more than anything."

Sammy snuggled her head into her mom's shoulder. Without realizing, her hand began stroking Jack's soft ears. He sighed, uncurled a little and laid his head on Sammy's knee.

It was probably a trick of the moonlight, but for a moment Sammy thought she glimpsed Papa Jack's shadow in the doorway. She smiled and felt herself drift off to sleep.

Always, she thought. We'll be together always.

232   Susan Brown

And now a Sneak Peek at

Not Yet Summer

Shuttled from one foster home to another, Marylee has never belonged anywhere. When she finds an abandoned baby, she is determined not to ever let April feel as unloved as she has. In desperation, she cons Petey, another neglected kid, into helping her raise the baby.

But what kind of life can she give April really? And what is happening to Petey? Marylee never knew that loving could hurt so much.

A new edition of the best-selling book from Scholastic.

Dragons of Frost and Fire

"I know she's still alive!"

A year ago her mother disappeared in an Alaskan blizzard, but Kit Soriano refuses to give up. Against all logic, propelled by recurring dreams of ice-white dragons and a magical silver knife, Kit journeys to the wilderness town of Silver Claw where her mother vanished. She's clearly not welcome, but her knife throbs with heat and her dreams show the impossible – mythical dragons are guarding her sleeping mother.

Desperate, Kit has no choice but to rely on Dai, who knows more than he says about the wild magic rippling beneath the surface of the town. She wants to trust him. But is he her friend or an enemy? If she's wrong, will she too be lost forever in the unforgiving Alaskan wilderness?

An exciting tale of adventure, love, and magic.

Not Yet Summer

by

Susan Brown

Chapter One

Marylee

When the alarm clock went off, Marylee slapped it with her hand, then lay back, trying to recapture the haven of sleep. There had been a dream – a rare thing of happiness and warmth. It lingered in her consciousness like beads of sunlight strung out in a haze, warming and drawing her. If she could just sleep awhile longer....

"Marylee!" Mrs. Watson rapped sharply on the door to her bedroom. "Get up. I heard that alarm, so there's no use pretending you didn't. You'd better not be late for school again!"

Marylee heard her walking briskly down the hall and pictured her squat form, her small-featured face. Her foster mother's face was routinely kind, but somehow it never warmed to affection.

Reluctantly Marylee opened her eyes. She stared at the blue wall with the framed magazine picture of a boy hauling in a fish from a foaming stream.

It was one of the two things in the room she really cared for – in spite of the grinning boy. The rest of the room was like the intent of the picture – square, dull and boyish. The Watsons had always had boys as foster children before, and the room was still impersonally geared to the male gender. The only concession to her sex was the bouquet of artificial flowers hastily stuck in one corner.

Except for the boy's intrusion into the scene, the picture evoked a wild freedom that Marylee longed for. There were old trees, some bent, some upright, all crowding down to the stream. The water gurgled and rushed over the rocks, foaming around the jagged edges. Way off in the background were mountains, misty blue and solitary.

Once, between foster homes, Marylee had been sent to a camp in country like that – a magic time. Her raging soul had emptied into the laughing water, and the twisting hurt and loneliness had drifted away into a haze. The silent trees had crowded close, feeling warm and loving when she stretched her childish arms around them. She had never cared for the lifelessness of her doll after that – after she had hugged the cool, living warmth of the great trees.

And the counselor had not told Marylee she was odd when she had whispered that she imagined the trees as people who would love her and sweep down their leaves to hug her. The gentle woman had smiled, and three days later had given her a book about four children who had found a country where trees walked and animals talked. She still had the book, ragged now from her love of it, carefully placed in the locked box where she kept her few treasures.

But the camp had been almost six years ago, when she was only eight – when her short, weak leg had simply made her feel miserably different from the other people who drifted into and out of her life. She had been too young then to realize that her lameness was a curse, the reason she was always alone, always alone and hated.

"Marylee!" Mrs. Watson called sharply. "For heaven's sake, are you going to get up?"

Marylee's lips pursed as familiar hatred drove the old memories away. Resentfully she pulled herself up and finally lurched out of bed. She was hungry. Might as well get up and eat.

But first she paused to examine the pale green flower shoots in the plastic pot balanced on the narrow window ledge. Marylee had filled the pot with earth from the garden as soon as the ground had thawed, almost a month ago. Before long the small shoots would bud and then flower.

A slight smile, stiff because it so rarely appeared, hovered on her lips. She loved small, growing things, things she could care for and make blossom. Once someone had said that she had "a way" with her. Marylee still cherished that stray compliment.

The kitchen smelled good when she finally limped downstairs. Pancakes and sausages, she noted with a tinge of pleasure. Mrs. Watson was a good cook, and as people went, she wasn't too bad. She talked too much about Marylee's limp, but at least she didn't look away or drip sickening pity over her, as most people did.

Once Marylee had thought the people cared and had been merely embarrassed by their reactions. But as little incident had piled on little incident over the years, her naive hopes about people had been worn away, leaving only a cynical hatred of them all.

"Good morning," Mrs. Watson said, too brightly.

Marylee sat down wordlessly and helped herself from the heaped plates on the table.

"There's something I have to talk to you about, dear," Mrs. Watson began after an uncomfortable pause.

Marylee looked up at her for a moment and clenched her jaw slightly. She hated that false word, "dear." When people called her that, they never meant it.

Nervously Mrs. Watson wiped her hands on a towel.

"Mr. Watson and I have talked about this a lot lately, so I don't want you to think it's a hasty decision. Or a personal one either," she added, with an embarrassed titter that was foreign to her normal manner. "But we feel we're really too old to continue parenting as we have in the past. We want to live our lives more for our own enjoyment now – travel a bit, get prepared for our retirement. So I'm afraid we'll have to give you up. We've already told Mrs. Wojansky of our decision, and the Children's Aid are trying hard to find a new home for you. I hope you understand our position, dear...."

There was a long, cold pause as, fork suspended halfway to her mouth, Marylee stared at her foster mother.

"Yeah, sure. Why not?" she said loudly, indifferently.

Deliberately she resumed eating, trying to ignore the sick feeling of fear churning in her stomach. Another home – another set of people to discover how much they really didn't like her.

I hate them. I hate them.... The words ground through her mind. But she had to seem normal. She had to go upstairs, brush her teeth, collect her books and sweater.

She found herself counting everything – the number of times the toothbrush slid over her teeth, the number of steps she took to cross the hall and enter her room, the number of papers she flipped through to find her homework page.

One, two, three, four, five... one, two, three... one... one...

Fiercely she bit her lip and forced her mind away from the monotonous drone of the number counting – her instinctive refuge from the searing hurt that was boiling up in her throat.

Oh, how she hated them....

"Time to go to school," Mrs. Watson called up the stairs. "Don't forget to take a sweater. It's not summer yet."

Numbly Marylee picked up her sweater and backpack and left for school.

The spring sun shone at an angle through the broken window of the warehouse, making Marylee's shadow strangely long and distorted on the debris-strewn floor. She didn't notice, however. Her eyes were shut, her body hugged to herself as she tried to raise memories of that beautiful warm forest and stream.

Aspens shiver, red maples wave,
While I and my enemies lie
Still
In the grave.

She shivered with melancholy pleasure at the poem she had made up. But she would have to go soon. They would all be looking for her.

"So who cares!" she whispered, tossing her head so the straight strands of brown hair slid over her shoulders for a moment before they drooped back around her face. She hugged herself tighter, relishing the feelings of hate that had soared through her that morning at school.

The sun, unusually hot and bright for the last day of March, was beating down on the asphalt of the school yard. Marylee leaned back against the wall of the school so that the shadows shrouded her slightly.

A group of girls had organized a game of skipping. Normally they would have felt themselves too mature to indulge in such a childish game, but the sunshine and the fresh air had raised their spirits. A hint of wistfulness grew in Marylee's mind as she watched them. Angela had a new outfit – another of the many things her parents showered on her curly blonde head. She was in the center of the girls now, laughing merrily.

As usual, they ignored Marylee.

She wondered what it would be like to be included in everything the gang did. Well, maybe she'd give it a try. A week or two more – a month at the most – and she'd be gone anyway.

She pulled herself upright and stared at the other girls. Taking a deep breath, she limped toward them, chin lifted. In a moment Marylee stood beside her giggling classmates, waiting stiffly for someone to acknowledge her presence. No one said anything.

"I want to play," she announced loudly.

The other girls looked at her in embarrassment. One of the gushy ones regarded Marylee's leg with obvious pity. "Do you think you should?"

"I want to play!" Marylee repeated in staccato tones.

"You can't just barge in where you haven't been invited. Jeez, are you rude!" Angela remarked, placing her hands on her hips and glaring at Marylee.

"It's a free country," Marylee said defiantly, breathlessly. "If I want to play, I can."

There was a cold pause. Miserably, Marylee realized she had done it all wrong – but there was no way to back down or to smooth over her presence.

"All right, if you want to play," Angela snapped, "then play!" She threw one end of the long skipping rope to another girl, so that Marylee was in the center. Then she began turning the rope.

Desperately Marylee hopped, trying to keep her balance despite her bad leg. Once, twice she managed to jump the rope. But Angela twisted it faster and faster and the rope began slapping Marylee's ankles as it turned first one way and then another.

"You wanted to play," Angela taunted. "Well, play then!"

Marylee stood still, frozen, as the rope snapped painfully across her skin. The circle of giggling girls closed in on her, snickering louder and louder. Marylee's hate churned up, pounded in her head, and finally broke loose.

She grabbed the swinging rope, jerking it out of the girls' hands. Then she shoved Angela, hard. Angela staggered slightly and Marylee pounced on her, pushing and shoving, finally tripping her.

"I'll show you!" Marylee shouted wildly, bouncing heavily onto Angela's stomach. "Have some dirt! It suits you!"

Gleefully she rubbed handfuls of dirt and gravel into Angela's clothes, all the while jabbing at her with her knees.

"Stop it! Stop it!" Angela shrieked. Her eyes were streaming with tears. The other girls stood in a circle, openmouthed and unmoving.

"Bitch! Bitch! Bitch!" Marylee screamed in glorious, roaring hate.

Then suddenly she felt someone pulling on her arms. The roaring died slightly. A teacher yanked Marylee roughly to her feet.

"What's going on here?" she demanded furiously, shaking Marylee's arm. "Who started this?"

"Marylee did!"

"Marylee started it! She shoved Angela down!" "She called her a bitch!"

"She rubbed dirt all over Angela and we couldn't stop her!"

"Marylee!"

The sun was low now, the shadows almost melted. Marylee's shorter, weaker leg had begun to feel numb. Cautiously she flexed her toes, waiting for the pins-and-needles feeling of returning circulation.

I'll take another look at my garden, she told herself. No way she would run home for them.

The garden was a patch of sandy soil where the concrete had broken up. Marylee had spent long, painful hours carrying the heavy chunks of cement to where she could dump them into the sluggish green water of the stream. Her limp had become worse from the strain.

But she had a garden all her own. No one else knew the feel of that coarse sand-dirt, or the rich smell of good peat moss and fertilizer worked into the soil. In her mind she could smell and feel every particle of the ground she was making come alive. Soon there would be flowers – something beautiful left behind even after they sent her to a new foster home.

Well, she could spend lots of time nursing the ragged patch of earth now – the principal had suspended her. There was a lot of talk which had floated by her exhausted indifference. Telephone calls, too. Everyone was informed – Mrs. Wojansky, her case manager, and the Watsons, her soon-not-to-be foster parents.

There were many solemn words, heavy pauses, and meaningful noises from the principal's mouth. Marylee paid no attention;

it didn't matter. Then he told her to go get her things and wait on the bench in the outer office.

She just shrugged at him and tried to saunter casually out of the office. But instead, she limped, her weak leg making the harsh *shuuing* sound she hated. She limped down the empty halls, hearing lonely echoes of other kids in their classes. Once she had retrieved her backpack and sweater, she had slipped out a back entrance and walked to the warehouse – her warehouse. No one knew she came here.

"Who would care anyhow?" she muttered defiantly as she limped across the floor toward the small window. Who cares about *anything*, she thought as she put her head out the square, glassless hole. She folded her elbows on the sill, peered down at the worked soil of her garden below and then out at the smelly stream only a few yards away.

Maybe once you were a real brook, she thought, not all poisoned and crippled by the cement. A real brook....

A shrill bark pierced the quiet. A dog! A dog had trotted up and was digging at her garden, ripping out her seeds!

"Stop! Get away!" Marylee shrieked. She beat her arms, trying desperately to slap the dog away. But the window was too high.

Frantically, she looked around for help. A boy with a lean face and uncombed hair was standing a short distance away, grinning and sipping on a carton of milk.

"Stop him! Please!" she pleaded.

But he just shrugged and stood by indifferently while the dog tore into her seeds.

Dragons of Frost and Fire

by

Susan Brown

ONE

The floatplane touched down on Silver Lake, spewing sheets of water into the air. Pressing her icy hands against the passenger window, Kit Soriano tried to force back a shudder. This far north, the Rocky Mountains peaks thrust into the sky like teeth – old teeth, cruel teeth, with glacial lips pulled back into a snarl.

"Silver Claw," the pilot called over his shoulder. "Last stop of humanity."

David Soriano peered out his own window, then reached his hand across the seat to grip his daughter's cold fingers. Silently they stared at this terrible place where they had come to find answers. Beyond the narrow beach, a few weather-beaten buildings made up the town. Past that, mountainous ice caps blended into clouds in every direction. At the north end of the lake, a glacier hundreds of feet high lay between the mountains like a mythic sleeping monster. Aqua and blue ice shone translucent in the sunlight.

"This is what mom tried to describe...." Kit gripped the dragonshaped knife hidden in her pocket – she was going to need every ounce of magic her mother had said it possessed. There was nothing else left for her to believe in.

The pilot eased the plane to the dock and cut the engine. Kit's ears still thrummed with the vibrations, when a series of rumbles and cracks rolled across the lake and through the skin of the plane. An ice monolith slowly split from the glacier and crashed into the water. Spray shot a hundred feet into the air. Shock waves raced across the lake, rocking the plane.

When Kit gasped and clutched the armrests, the pilot laughed. "That's Silver Snake Glacier." He pointed to the ice cliff. "In spring it breaks up some — calving, it's called. But you've never heard anything like the roars and howls that come from that ice snake in winter. I was holed up here one year when an early blizzard rolled in. I swear I thought the noise alone would kill me."

Kit forced herself to stare impassively at the forbidding Alaskan landscape. "I'm not afraid of noise." She would not, would not let this place defeat her.

The pilot shrugged. "Hope you're not planning to stay too long," he warned. "Once winter gets her talons into this country, it can cost you your life to go outside of town."

"We'll be back in New York by winter," her father said. "We're only staying a couple of weeks."

Until we find her, Kit vowed.

The pilot heaved himself out of his chair, wrestled with the door, and showed them how to scramble down to the pontoon and then jump onto the dock. Kit shivered. Even though it was mid-August, the Alaskan air was cold through her fleece vest. She warmed up a little as they unloaded their gear.

A dozen of the town's residents drifted down to the dock, but Kit kept her eyes off the kids. Those kids had lured her mother to Silver Claw – nearly a quarter of them were albino, a genetic mutation. Dr. Nora Reits had been a genetics researcher. Nearly a year ago she had disappeared without a trace in an early fall storm in Silver Claw.

Kit again touched the silver pocketknife nestled in her pocket. Magic find her, she prayed silently. Warmth tingled against her skin – the connection was still strong. Relieved, Kit turned her energy to separating their gear from the supplies ordered by the residents.

A lot of folks were on the dock now. In spite of herself, Kit sneaked a look under her lashes. The albino kids had snow-white hair and glacier blue eyes. Unlike some albino people, their sparkling glances showed good eyesight and they glowed with health.

"Dr. Soriano?" A big man with red hair stuck out his hand to Kit's father. "I'm Pat Kelly, mayor of this place. I wish I could welcome you here under better circumstances."

Dr. Soriano shook hands with the mayor. "We appreciate your willingness to let us get some closure on my wife's disappearance."

The mayor nodded. "I understand your feelings. We lost one of our own boys in that blizzard. This is a hard land – beautiful, but hard."

"Yes," Dr. Soriano said gazing at the ring of jagged peaks. "But I'm hoping the clinic will be a useful return for your hospitality."

"My mother-in-law will keep you busy, even if no one else does," Pat replied with an easy smile. "It's a long flight to Anchorage when the problems are the aches and pains old folks feel every time the weather changes."

As Kit reached up to grab the rest of their bags, she drew a deep breath. After all the setbacks and problems, she could hardly believe they were really here.

It had taken her father weeks to work out their journey. Getting to Silver Claw would be no problem – a regular flight from New York City to Anchorage and then they could book seats on the floatplane that delivered supplies to the town every couple of weeks. But inquiries about where to stay had been discouraging. There was apparently no reliable Internet connection that far north, and so all communication was by snail mail. A letter from the town council, signed Mary McGough, Secretary, had been brusque. The council regretted there was no hotel in Silver Claw.

Dr. Soriano's lips had thinned as he read the letter aloud to Kit.

"Isn't she the person Mom rented a room and office from? Wasn't it above a store or something?" Kit had asked.

"Yup," her dad said. "Let's try this one more time." That evening, he wrote back politely requesting that he and his daughter rent the room that his wife had previously occupied.

Three weeks later a second response from the town secretary stated that she was using the space Dr. Reits had rented for storage and so it was no longer available.

"I don't think they want us," Dr. Soriano had told his daughter over macaroni and cheese.

"I don't care. You promised me..." Kit looked challengingly into his eyes.

"And I keep my promises," he'd said. "Have some salad. It's only a little brown."

After dinner, while Kit had loaded the dishwasher and then tackled physics homework, he had written a third letter to the town council.

Dear Members of the Council,

I am hoping that we will still be able to work out the details of my daughter's and my visit. We are coming to Silver Claw. As east coast city people we don't have a lot of experience with wilderness camping, but we will come with tents and backpacks and set up on the glacier itself, if necessary.

However, I have a proposal for you. I am a medical doctor and I'm willing to operate a free clinic for the residents of the area in return for accommodation and supplies while my daughter and I are in town.

We will be arriving on August 12th, with or without a place to stay.

Sincerely,
David Soriano, M.D.

The next response came from Pat Kelly instead of the secretary and it was a lot friendlier. A new cabin had been built for his family and he was willing to let Kit and her dad use it for a couple of weeks. He sympathized with the Soriano's need to see the town where Dr. Reits had spent her last few weeks. The residents of the town would be pleased to welcome them.

Kit and her dad flew from New York on August 11th, spent the night in Anchorage and the next morning boarded the small floatplane.

After all her thinking and worrying, it seemed to Kit that she was in a dream as she stood at the edge of the dock and gazed across the wild landscape. The glacier glinted, shifting colors like a living, crystal animal.

Mayor Kelly turned from Dr. Soriano to the people standing on the dock behind him. "Here, you kids give a hand. Kirsi...Dai...grab some of the bags."

Two of the older albino teenagers, a girl and boy, left the group. Both were tall and strong, their white-blonde hair ruffling in the steady breeze. They radiated health and were incredibly good looking. Mesmerized, Kit realized with a small shock that they were better than good looking – they were the most beautiful teens she had ever seen. They were graceful, perfectly proportioned, and there wasn't even a zit to be seen. Kit thought she could hate them just for that.

As Kirsi leaned down to pick up luggage, she turned cold blue eyes toward Kit. "You shouldn't have come here," she hissed. "You soft city people don't belong." She hoisted the heavy pack over her shoulder with ease and strode away without a backward glance.

The breeze off the lake quickened. Kit shivered.

"You'll get used to the temperatures," Dai said beside her. He appeared about seventeen, a year older than she was. Up close, Kit thought his looks alone could warm her up.

Kit made a grab for her peace of mind and shrugged. "I'm not afraid of the cold."

"That's good because sometimes we get a lot of it. I'm Dai Phillips." He stuck out his hand to shake.

Kit hesitated a split second, then shook his hand. It was so very warm and firm. A responding flash of heat shot through her. This was not normal for her at all.

"I'm Kit." At home the kids either didn't touch or did hand slaps and fist bumps. Nobody under forty shook hands.

Patrick Kelly picked up one of Dr. Soriano's medical cases. "We do appreciate your willingness to run a health clinic even for two weeks, Doc," he said. "Hey there, Jancy. You, Mikey. Help the doctor with his bags." Two red-haired children each picked up a suitcase.

"Dai, are you going to stand around all day or are you going to help that little girl out?"

Hot color flushed Dai's face. "Yes, Uncle Pat," he said under his breath. He reached for a duffel. "This yours, Kit?"

"I'll get it," she said. "I packed it. I can carry it." She hoisted it up and over her thin shoulder. "And I'm sixteen...not a little girl." She knew she looked too young and fragile to be in the wilderness. But she also knew that her slender bones were connected to tough muscle.

"Okay," Dai said. "But it's a bit of a hike to the cabin and I'm used to the path."

"Whatever." Kit slid the bag back to the dock, refusing to allow even a flicker of relief to cross her face. She'd jammed it with everything she thought might be useful – survival gear, guidebooks, contour maps, compass, and a Swiss Army knife.

Dai's deep blue eyes searched her own.

"What?" Kit demanded. His intense gaze unnerved her.

Dai leaned over and lifted the bag like it weighed six ounces instead of sixty pounds. "It's good you've come to us — you're the kind that's called."

"Called? Called what?"

"Called by the mountains and wilderness. By the heart that beats up there." Again, his eyes pierced her own. "Your mother was the same. You both belong here. I feel it."

Kit felt a lump rise sharply in her throat so she turned away and stared at the town as though fascinated by the worn clapboard structures. Kirsi stood at the top of the path, arms folded, looking stonily down at the people on the dock. Kit stared back defiantly.

"My mother didn't belong here and I don't either," she turned and told Dai. "I'm going to find out what happened to her and then you'll never see me again."

She picked up a bag and marched up the path toward Kirsi. Other men and children took the rest of the luggage. The remainder of the people finished unloading boxes of supplies from the plane and began hauling them up the hill toward town. Dai strode after her, whistling off-key. Kit glanced back at him. She had never seen anyone so vibrantly alive. And he had talked about her mother. Had he gotten to know her? Would he have information that would lead Kit to her?

Abruptly she slowed down, matching her steps to his. But with a cool glance, he trudged faster away from her, still whistling. Kit's eyes narrowed, but she followed without comment. In a moment she had reached Kirsi. The girl looked her over like she was a dead fish washed onto the shore.

"Stay away from Dai. He has no use for your kind," Kirsi mocked.

"What kind is that, Kirsi?" Kit demanded.

The girl's lips curled into a sneer. "A weak outlander. You'll be very sorry you ever came here." She shoved past Kit, knocking her off balance.

Regaining her footing, Kit glared after her. "I think you will be surprised." She made no effort to catch up, waiting instead for her dad and the others.

"The house is this way, Doctor." Mayor Kelly gestured along an overgrown dirt road that edged the lake. "The clinic building is in town, but this cabin has an incredible view of Silver Snake."

The cabin sat on a rounded hill overlooking the lake. The building was made of shaped logs, with a fresh look about them. Shuttered windows along the sides were wide and evenly spaced. A long porch was angled to face the glacier.

Everyone trooped through the screen door, but Kit dropped her bag and leaned on the railing, looking towards mountains and ice. Behind her, voices filled the cabin. But out here, the stillness folded into a sense of being on the edge of another world. Kit breathed deeply, tasting the tang of wilderness, and another acrid scent — sweet and bitter mingled. She tossed her head to let the clean air wash over her. After the long despair, she was coming alive again. Kit remembered how her mother had described this place in her letters...

Silver Snake Glacier drapes the mountains like a huge sleeping animal. It really seems alive, shifting with every color that ever existed. I hope you get to see it some day – it must be one of the wonders of the world! I am going to hike up there and see if I can fathom its secrets. Something that otherworldly must have secrets, Kit. Devin tells me the glacier is riddled with crevasses and caves – a beautiful but deadly creature, I guess. It wakes when the winter storms howl over the mountains....

Dai came out on the porch and stood beside her. Despite herself, Kit was too aware of the warmth he radiated. Of those broad shoulders and lithe build. She'd never been this aware of the boys at home. Pheromones. He must be radiating mutated pheromones and she was feeling every one of them.

Another crack shattered the quiet of the town.

"Loud, isn't it?" Kit said turning to him. She froze. His eyes were a deeper blue. She'd swear they had darkened. Ridiculous. Even weird eyes, genetically mutated eyes, shouldn't change color. It had to be a trick of the light.

"This is a great time of year to be in Silver Claw." Dai's expression once again lightened to an easy smile. "There's hiking, hunting and fishing during the day and bonfires and get-togethers at night. Mary McGough at the general store gets in movies now and then."

"Sounds terrific," Kit said, "but I already have plans." She forced herself to turn away from those hot, mesmerizing eyes and look back at the cold waters of the lake. Her mother had said native legends put some kind of mythic beast in those cold depths.

Then Dai's hand, hot and strong, gripped her arm. "There are no other plans in Silver Claw," Dai told her. "You'll be smart to listen to me." The warning in his voice was unmistakable.

"Or what?" Kit challenged. How friendly or how dangerous was this guy? He was like fire and ice. Already this place was freaking her out, all beauty and danger.

His eyes shifted even darker, making that weird sense of warmth flare through her again. She didn't know whether he would have answered or not because they were interrupted by the door swinging open. The moment bled away.

"Kit," her dad called. "Which bedroom do you want?"

"Excuse me," Kit stepped past Dai and followed her father.

Inside, several men and women had settled on the sofas and chairs. Dai came in after her and crossed over to Kirsi who leaned against the far wall. As they stood talking in quiet voices and sometimes glancing in her direction, Kit felt another surge of anger. Were they talking about her? And why should she care?

In the meantime, two women were opening and shutting the cupboard doors in the kitchen area, calling on Dr. Soriano to admire how thoroughly they had stocked up for him.

"My wife is bringing some lasagna over," the mayor said. "A bit of a welcome to let you get yourself unpacked and settled tonight."

"Dr. Soriano," Dai struck in, "my mother said I'm to ask you for dinner tomorrow at seven, if you don't have other plans...." He glanced mockingly at Kit.

"Great," Dr. Soriano said. "That's very kind. We'll be there. Now Kit, what about that bedroom?"

Three bedrooms opened off the kitchen-dining-living area, so Kit chose one where the window faced the glacier. While her dad chatted with the people who had helped bring their belongings up, Kit hauled in her bags. Methodically, she unpacked her clothing and filled the drawers of the wooden dresser. She left all her survival gear in the duffel bag, zipped it up, and pushed it far under the bed.

"Kit!" her dad called. "The most marvelous dinner is being spread out here for us!"

The main room was packed with big, loud strangers. It seemed like everyone who had come down to the dock had migrated up to the cabin and brought a few friends along. Did any of those open, friendly faces hide the secret of her mother's disappearance? She wanted to shout at them, demand they tell her what they knew, but instead she forced herself to paste on a fake smile.

"Please, you must stay," her father was urging.

With only a brief show of reluctance, everyone dug into the lasagna, salad, bread and meat that all seemed to have magically appeared. Kit picked among the dishes and settled in the remotest corner of the sofa. Dai left Kirsi and perched on the arm beside her. Ignoring him, Kit took a bite of the dark meat. Flavor exploded in her senses.

"Backstrap," Dai said. "The tenderest and tastiest part of a moose."

Kit put her fork down but chewed on. It was good — different from anything else she'd tasted. "Great!" she mumbled through her full mouth.

"You're honored," Dai said. "That's probably the last of Uncle Pat's winter store. He's the best hunter in town, but we try to only hunt moose in the fall and winter."

Kit cut another piece of meat and popped it in her mouth. "The only moose I ever saw for real was in a zoo. It was big and sad looking so it seems cruel to hunt them."

"We have to eat and there aren't many fast food restaurants in the wilderness," Dai replied. "Besides, those hamburgers don't come from carrots."

Kit took a big bite of her bread to avoid answering. She knew he was right, but she didn't want to acknowledge that the rules were different here in Silver Claw. With mountains, lakes and glaciers surrounding them, they hunted to eat. They killed to survive.

A burst of laughter filled the cabin. She tried another bite of backstrap. It tasted fine on her tongue. Kit looked around at all the handsome, strong faces. She would learn what they knew, she vowed. And if they had secrets, she would find them.

Despite their protests about letting the Sorianos unpack, the townspeople didn't leave for hours. By the time Kit could finally get to bed, she was too wound up to sleep.

Outside, twilight had eased over the land, casting the mountains into dark relief. The luminous hands on her watch read 11:03 but the sky still shone dusky blue. Kit sat on her bed, wrapped in a quilt, looking out toward Silver Snake Glacier.

It drew her, called her, just as Dai had said it would. Her mom's letters had described the hours she spent hiking by the glacier. She wrote that the sight and sound of the ancient ice relieved her frustrations when the townspeople refused to cooperate with her research.

And that's how I'll start, Kit decided; she would go to the places her mother had described, try to find some kind of clue her mother may have left behind. Looking out the open window at the immense distances and peaks, Kit wondered with a sinking heart whether she would be able to find the places from the descriptions in the letters. In New York, hemmed in by buildings and streetlights, she had not been able to grasp the vastness of the landscape.

Her father came in, set a lantern on the table beside her bed and sat down.

"They seem like nice people around here," he said at last.

Kit rolled her eyes. "That's what Mom said...until they found out what she was doing."

Her hand slipped under her pillow to touch the knife and the packet of letters. In the last one, Nora Reits had written in an excited scrawl from her office over the general store. She had said she would try to slip the letter into the outgoing mail sack before the floatplane arrived. This flight, she was sure, would bring lab results for the blood samples she had coaxed from one albino boy. Kit got the letter two days after her mother disappeared.

"Kit, it was a simple hiking accident," her dad said. "You know she hiked up there alone, even though the weather was threatening."

"Then why did the lab results disappear?" Kit demanded. "And the searchers didn't find a body. They're keeping her somewhere. I know it! My knife...."

"Kit, don't start about that knife again."
Her father rubbed his hand over his face; his
eyes were exhausted. Kit fell silent.

If only he would believe what Kit knew
against all reason was true. Her mother was
alive.

Another crack reverberated through the
air. The lantern flickered. Somewhere, out
there, Kit knew her mother was alive.

ABOUT THE AUTHOR

Adventure, mystery, and magic propel Susan Brown, fuelling her imagination into writing more and more stories for her favorite audience of kids and teens.

Susan lives with her two border collie rescue dogs amid wild woods and overgrown gardens in Snohomish, Washington. From there she supervises her three daughters, assorted sons-in-law and two grandsons. It's a great way to be a writer!

Find more information, free stories,
and news about upcoming books at:
www.susanbrownwrites.com

Susan is also one half of Stephanie Browning, the pen name shared with her writing partner of close to a thousand years, Anne Stephenson.
www.stephaniebrowningromance.com

68194217R10159

Made in the USA
Lexington, KY
05 October 2017